THERE'S A HOLE
IN MY *soul*

GEORGE ALLEN

For Mom. I will never forget...

CONTENTS

ACKNOWLEDGEMENTS

The book is a work of fiction, but with many truths in it. Many true life experiences that I have taken from my own experience, and I have used some experiences from others to bring the work of fiction together. Where people may associate themselves with characters in this book, this is coincidental, but it may be that an experience that I had with you prompted the narrative, and I thank each and every one of you for making it possible to write this work of fiction.

So many people have left an indelible mark in my life. My life would have been so much poorer had you not been part of it. As there are too many people to thank personally, I will, however, say thank you to a handful of special people who remain special and part of my life throughout this journey:

Mom. May God provide you with the eternal peace you so richly deserve. I will love you until the end of my days.

Liza. My sister, my rock, who accepts me with all my flaws. Unconditionally.

Kayla. My niece but so much so my very own child. I cannot think how life had been before your arrival. Somehow, it feels as if you have been part of me for all my life.

Bennie. The best mate one could ever hope for in life. Who understands me and through it all still is willing to be my best friend. That is a feat in itself!

Ronel. The best and truest lady friend one could ever hope for in life. Who never judges me, not even when I stumble.

Trudie. Clorets. Words cannot describe how strong our bond of friendship has been. For many years. And many more to come.

Knoffelma. Anna-Louise. Ale. Antjie. Annabelle. Love you always.

Oupa Ben, Marlo, Luben, Marise. My second precious family. Your love and support mean the world to me.

Zhanie. Bobble-bobble will always have a special place in my heart, as only you and I could do it.

Ané, Angelique, Basil, Barbara, Belinda, Bev, Bokkie, Bongani, Celeste, Charmain, Dagmar, Denise, Dewet, Ema, Gary, Gill, Glenn, Heinz, Jenni, Karen, Kathy, Kelvin, Khungeka, Leoni, Lindsay, Lizelle, Marisca, Marleen, Marliza, Meera, Mia, Michelina, Mike, Mothusi, Neo, Nicole, Patrice, Petrizia, Pule, Raganee, Rasagna, Renata, Renee, Riyaad, Rose, Rudolph, Selvam, Shereen, Sheral, Thami, Theo, Venita, Verlene, Yogeshree, Wayne, Welna. For staying in touch, caring and extending a wonderful hand of friendship, long after my departure.

To all my remaining work colleagues – the Fleet Management and PeopleFirst teams. And the Standard Bankers that supported and believed in me. You are simply too many to name in fear that I might inadvertently omit to thank you. You all know who you are…

And last but definitely not least, to Anthea, Adrienne and Theunis. You make every Saturday breakfast a joyous event and a culinary feast.

Prologue

Faggot, faggot! Nancy boy's a faggot! Faggot, faggot! Sissy boy's a faggot!

With a cold sweat and an involuntary shudder, I awake from my dream, only remembering flashes as the last remnants of the dream start to fade. It is a cold Saturday winter's morning when I was so rudely awakened by this chant in my dream. Lying in bed, fully awake now, listening to the sound of my rapid heartbeat keeping rhythm with the sound of the icy raindrops falling on the roof and on the balcony outside my bedroom. While lying in bed still, strangely disturbed by the dream, I heard a song playing on the radio in the background, competing with the incessant patter of the rain. When I heard the words "… there's a hole in my soul…" in the lyrics, I jolted upright in my bed. I immediately thought to myself that the song was talking to me, that no other words ever sang before, not in any prose or in any poem, other than those specific six words aptly described how I felt and in fact always have felt as a person. That even when I was a child as far back as I can remember I often wondered how many holes the soul could have. How much punishment and beatings the soul could take and when or how do these holes ever heal? Or do they simply remain holes forever, albeit as part of and attached to your soul and that over time the surface of these holes is healed but beneath it all, is a simmering volcano dormant for now, but able to at any time spew and erupt.

Relax, I told myself. The dream and the lyrics were merely coincidental and surely could not have anything to do with each other. I forced myself to turn around on my side and to lie down again in bed, facing the window, looking out at the cold winter rain. But doing this somehow caused me to listen more intently to the song playing in the background on the radio. Every time I heard those six words being sung, I felt chills and goosebumps all over me. And my mind started to drift away, drifting and contemplating the meaning and purpose of one's soul. That perhaps when you die one day and your soul goes up to heaven, will it then only be healed from its holes by the Lord, but until then, the soul is never complete, never whole again, as everyone on this earth at some point in time had a crush or a blow to their souls?

My friends call their pain, disappointments and failures heartache and they love to take the mickey out of me for the phrase that I use: I call it soul-ache, for every time they tease me, I ask them how often do they hear the phrase heart-destroying. No, soul-destroying is the phrase that is used. Our whole being is as a result of our souls; therefore, it is the soul that gets hurt, the soul that takes the damage. And yet, through it all, somehow the soul manages to survive and to persevere until our very last breath. The soul is probably, in my most humble opinion, the strongest and most enduring part of us, albeit that rumour has it that it weighs all of seven grams only. How strong, depends on each soul, and I suppose to some extent the size and number of holes blown into the soul, some leaving gaping holes as big as shotgun wounds whilst others leave tiny punctured holes and others mere scratch marks only. But for each hole, there is also a kind of soothing filling, closing the hole in a slow yet effective healing way. Sometimes, the hole is filled to the brim, leaving the cause and its effect behind, becoming a distant memory, fading into the twilight. But from time to time, it is the soul and those very holes that make us and form us into who we are today. When we do some soul-searching, introspection of the big kind (biggest kind?), we often have an epiphany and marvel on how a situation became a defining point in our lives.

And by listening to the lyrics of the song, I realised that for me, my soul has always been the one thing that I treasured and guarded the most. And respected the most. For my poor soul (pardon the pun!) took some beatings over the years, some self-inflicted but mostly as a result of life. Living it, taking what has been handed to it. See if I could make some lemonade from those lemons that life kept on hurling at me!

And while the last chords of the song faded in the background, the cold rain continuing to keep its own beat, I involuntarily started to take a melancholy leap down memory lane. And the leap took me to my childhood and soared and spanned over several decades, digging up memories long ago buried and until then I thought best stayed buried! Memories filled with holes, its causes, its potential remedies but mostly the beatings taken over time by my soul. And then once the leap was taken, I started to stroll down memory lane, reliving so many memories again. Strolling and soaring along, I realised not all my memories that caused holes in my soul were all tragic, sad or heartbreaking only. That in fact most bad memories also had a lighter and even at times a humorous side to it as well. That these memories may have certain perspectives to it, perspectives that I took from life experience. And reliving them now, the reality of what I experienced then may be different now, but the hole it created in my soul remains unfaltering. And omnipresent.

And on that cold and rainy Saturday morning, alone in bed, staring out the window, looking outwardly to the world, inwardly I started to relive my life from the time that I was a young boy who became a man, who started with nothing, came from nothing and who was determined to turn nothing into something. Not to the world. But to the boy who became a man who came from nothing.

The Soul Destroyers

The Holes of Poverty, Hunger and Humiliation

Strolling at a relatively fast pace down memory lane, my memory takes me back to the time of me being a young boy growing up in a small suburban town, known for its poverty, for its domestic disputes and for most of its inhabitants, its poor folk. When people asked you where you were from, you never mentioned the town by name as immediately people would get the wrong idea and form an everlasting and wrong opinion of you and the town and its occupants. The town's people were good

11

people, of good stock and of integrity, but outcasts due to living in poverty. So you best shied away and tried to hide where you came from, or so I believed everyone did. To my surprise in later years I would learn that I was possibly the only one too shy to admit where I was from, too shy to admit this was my background, that I was poor, that I was possibly from a poor class family and that I was born into it, whether I liked it or not. However, if there was a railway track close to our little suburban town, it wouldn't have mattered on which side of the railway track you stayed, as it would always be perceived as growing up on the wrong side of the train tracks!

Tranquillity. That was the name of our town, now long forgotten and in tatters and ruins – but at the time in the early seventies a small suburban town surrounded (more like flanked!) by several other suburbs as well. To the west, we had Tranquillity Park, to the north Relay Park, to the east Fisher Fountain and to the south Sunset View. Right in the middle of all of this was our tiny little poverty-stricken suburb. And albeit that Tranquillity lived up to its name in its appearance, in our home we often craved tranquillity, which was seldom present.

The suburb had several streets that ran horizontally and far fewer streets vertically hooking up and creating intersections. We lived in a tiny house that was first rented from the local municipality by my grandmother and when my grandmother passed away, we moved into the house and continued renting it from the local municipality. I remember that the house was located on Serene Street. Serenity, tranquillity, such names conflicting with the lives of its townspeople.

"Mom, why do we live in Tranquillity?" I one day asked Mom.

"This is the place where your grandmother was born and grew up and this is where I was born and raised. I know of no other place that I will rather be, my son."

For a young boy, this answer seemed good enough. Sitting outside in the street, I looked at our house. Our house, light blue painted walls on the outside with a painted red corrugated zinc roof and cream coloured walls on the inside was little more than the size of a dollhouse that had electricity but had no hot running water, as there were no geyser or bath or shower facilities at all.

"Mom, why is it that our house only has an outside toilet?" I interrupted Mom again.

"Ours most surely is not!" Mom answered me indignantly.

But it is, I thought to myself. I have seen our neighbours' houses; they all have their toilets inside. For us, the ablution facility was outside in the backyard, covered in a corrugated tin hut that was roughly erected around the throne to provide a false sense of privacy. The toilet, fortunately, could be flushed using a yank chain, but there was no electricity cabling that allowed for the switching on of any lights in the toilet. So, either a candle was used when there was a need to use the toilet at night, or the ablutions were done in the black of night. Thank goodness as a child, I had little need of using the ablution facilities at night, for walking the ten steps from the back door to the toilet entrance with a candle in hand always seemed like a journey into the Twilight Zone, never knowing what creatures are lurking, waiting to pounce on you. For the less urgent ablution requirements, a chamber pot, something little more than a tiny bucket would be used during the night. I preferred to think of it as a chamber pot, as somehow it sounded mystical, regal even and not downright poverty-stricken!

"Mom, I hate using this bucket. My aim is almost always out and then you are angry with me."

"Sit on the bucket then, as I have told you many times before," Mom would answer me.

"But no boy sits when he needs to pee!" I whined.

13

"Well, they don't miss now, do they?" Mom had me there, so it meant that either I had to improve on my aim, or I needed to sit. This all was fortunately done with some privacy. For the more urgent ablution needs, however, the candle had to be lit and the brave walk had to be taken for no urgent needs were accommodated or allowed to be done in the chamber pot! Mom simply refused to budge on that one!

Coming from the neighbours' house the next day after running an errand for them, I again noticed how different their house was to ours. Our house itself had only one single large bedroom, but for privacy and living purposes, it was divided into two bedrooms by simply placing two wardrobes standing in the middle of the room, creating an imagined and I supposed perhaps a false sense of having two separate bedrooms. As you entered the house from the rear to the left would be the kitchen, to the right the bedroom and to the front the lounge. Once you exited the lounge, you were on the front porch with three steps that took you out on the street.

Bathing took place in another bucket, in the privacy of your room, a different one thankfully and fairly bigger than the one used for ablutions, where hot water was first boiled in a kettle then poured into the bucket, followed with the right amount of cold water to make a soothing and not scathing wash. Once I was finished washing, I would call Mom who then would dispense of the soap water in the outside drain.

Mom would always ask me, "Let me see your ears?" as she wanted to make sure that I had washed behind my ears. This seemed to be the spot that I regularly missed.

"Now let me see those soles of your feet."

If the soles of my feet were not as scrubbed and clean as Mom would have liked them to be, she would then grab a brush and clean my feet for me before dispensing of the soapy water. This inevitably led to moments of hilarious laughter, as the brush tickled me and often I would play this game with Mom when my father was not around or out of earshot, knowing I am in for a good laugh.

"Look how dirty these feet still are. You again did not wash the soles as I have shown you. Come here, young man, let me give you a hand."

As a young boy, adventure was part of my imagination, standing in the backyard was an old avocado tree that carried fruit once every ten years and opposite the tree, a coal shed, however, as we had no coal stove the shed was merely used for storage. I often climbed the tree, sitting high in the branches to escape the realities of true life below.

"Come down from there." Many an evening Mom would call for me, either at dinner time or time for a wash.

"One day you are still going to hurt yourself," Mom cautioned.

"Leave the boy," my father said to Mom. "This is the only thing he ever does that I have seen other boys his age also do."

The look Mom gave my father never escaped me, but I was too far into my adventure to really understand what just took place between my parents. But, reality soon would come crashing down.

The front red porch was a sure sign that the house was ours, as it was made shiny and slippery with red Cobra polish, and I remember and marvel at how always more shiny and slippery our front porch was to the rest of the neighbours in our street. Mom's pride and joy! Our kids' greatest nightmare, for many times running and playing, would result in a slip that caused some serious bruising, but we never did listen as children, always running and playing, seemingly unaware of the red dangerous and slippery porch beneath our feet. The porch was never dull, always shiny and always looked freshly polished, as Mom took pride in what little we had at our disposal.

The roof of the house, painted red, on rainy days would make the pitter-patter of raindrops sound melodic and I would spend hours lying on my tummy at the open back door, watching and listening to the rain. Looking at the splashes of the raindrops, the melody of it all took me to places and fantasies that only a child can have and make. Using the toilet on these days was a very different story, for the corrugated tin shack and erection had tiny nail holes in it and a long visit to the throne could leave one dripping wet during a particular summer rainstorm. This was life, as I became to know it in our tiny suburb of Tranquillity.

Peaceful Street was the main hub of our town, and here you would find all kinds of stores ranging from three mini-supermarkets (more like cafés), furniture stores, clothing stores, butchery, vegetable store and rags and material stores. Mom was known to all these shop owners, as she had an account with each of them that she tried to settle as often as she could. The shop owners of Tranquillity understood the life of poverty most of its inhabitants lived and as they also lived in the same area, they trusted the community and knew that the debts would be settled.

As a child and right up to my years as a student, I frequented the one mini-supermarket often, which was owned by the local Portuguese family; José, a burly man with a short temper and Catia, his slightly overweight wife. I loved spending time at their café. Whenever I had some small change that I had saved up over several weeks to have a cold drink, I would run down to the shop and buy a two hundred and fifty millilitres bottle of Coke and sometimes, if I was especially lucky with the funds I saved, I could even buy a half litre!

Once finishing my cold drink, I would stock these by stashing and hiding the empty bottles in my duffel bag at home (or plastic bags if the duffel bag was for some unknown reason not available). This was to make sure that none of the neighbours or anyone else in the neighbourhood would see me walking and trading empty bottles for cash or supplies. Once I had enough empty glass bottles to return for cash (almost once every two months and sometimes once a month if I was particularly lucky), I would carry these bottles in the duffel bag to trade them. Off to José and Catia, I would rush, hoping for a few bob to buy either some more cold drinks or some food when I especially had quite a selection of empties. This was usually a toasted sandwich or fish and chips. Oily. Unhealthy. But oh so scrumptious. I had a special unspoken arrangement with Catia and José, and probably the only one of their patrons ever allowed behind the counter of their shop. When I arrived at José and Catia's, I would very quickly walk behind the counter into the back room and place these empties in empty crates.

"Ola, Catia! Ola, José!" I would greet them in my broken Portuguese.

"Ola, bambino. To the usual place." Catia would direct me as if by now I still did not know where to go or where to stack the empty bottles that I returned.

Catia or José then would calculate my reward and wow, what a rich boy I became, even if for only a few minutes on that day. So, I would frequent this shop quite often, making the step at the entrance of this café my personal space, watching life and how it is lived by strangers passing me by. José and Catia never once minded that I sat there and stared out in awe and wonderment at the world around me.

✳✳✳

Thinking of those steps brought back another snapshot of a happier time to me while the fragments of the dream still stuck in my cerebrum, the incessant rain and cold continue to take me down memory lane. It was on this very step that Mom several years later came running towards me.

"There was a phone call from one of the organisations you applied to for a permanent job. They want you to call them back," Mom excitedly shouted at me from the corner of the street.

The representative left a message with my aunt whose phone number was used, as we did not have money for any telecommunication facilities. It was an arrangement that worked well, as my aunt lived next door to where we stayed at the time. When I returned the call on that day, I received the overwhelming news that my interview and application for permanent work were resounding successes.

"Thank you, Lord!" went through my mind and I said it aloud, so thankful and happy that I am about to enter the adult world and start building a career. So, that step at that café has a special place in my heart.

Listening to the rain, I was quite surprised at being able to so vividly recall the emotions I went through on that day. But my mind inevitably kept wandering back to the earlier days, when I was still very young. For some reason, I was pulled towards facing my childhood again, all because of a dream, and all because of a song.

✳✳✳

José and Catia had two sons and a daughter – Jorge, Christiano and Alicia. When finished with their normal school days in an English school, off to Portuguese school the three of them would go as to ensure that they understood, read and write the Portuguese language as well as their parents do as well as in preparation for when they would eventually return to their motherland one day as adults. When done, after all the studying and homework was taken care of, they then had to work the remainder of the time in the café, packing goods, helping customers at the counter and generally ensuring that the business was taken care of. At times, they were allowed some time to play, and the four of us would play in the back yard and store room between all the empty boxes and crates. We would play hide and seek, cowboys and crooks and make a noise until Catia or José put a stop to the racket and the three of them had to return to resume their duties. Then I would return to my favourite spot, the front step of the café.

José and Catia had a special fondness for me, and I for them. When they had some family gatherings, they would often invite me along, and so I became a regular at their very irregular family functions. These functions could not be frequent as José and Catia had to continue making a living, but the times that they could get away, I was often with, enjoying fun and laughter with the rest of the family. So Catia and José became as much a part of Tranquillity and my life, growing up and experiencing life in Tranquillity.

One day at primary school the headmaster, Mr Lombard had a special announcement to make.

"Attention children. Attention children." He called us to order. "From time to time, our school is fortunate enough that the local television shows require children to be part of it, shows that I know you all watch on television like *Wheel the Wheel*, *Happy Hare* and *The Tubby Giant* and so on. So I am happy to let you all know that once again I am proud to announce that our very own local primary school was approached for a number of scholars to appear on television on *The Tubby Giant* show."

As always, our school was selected due to its location and neighbourhood and naturally fulfilled the requirement of selecting less privileged kids to experience life beyond the mundane.

19

At once, there was an outbreak of excitement and joyous laughter and chattering amongst the children. All we kids were so excited, we were going to be famous and rich or so we all dreamt.

"You must obtain consent; you must get the necessary permission from your parents. Also, only those scholars who have completed the consent forms and who have put up their names before the deadline date, will be selected out of this group of scholars," the headmaster continued once the noise levels subsided again.

It was made clear to us that only a small number of children would be accepted. That afternoon, I ran home as fast as I could and excitedly spoke to Mom and requested her to give me her permission that I could attend.

"Only if you are going to be a good boy and behave yourself, I don't want to be ashamed because of something my children did," Mom admonished.

"But I am always good. I will not make a fuss. I swear. Please, Mom!" I begged.

Mom relented and signed the slip, which I promptly returned to school the next day. Luckily, for me, I was one of the school kids selected. I was simply out of my mind. I was going to be on TV! I was going to be famous. I was going to be rich. Oh, how I waited for the time to arrive for us to go to the filming of the show. Finally, one Saturday morning we were picked up at school and taken to the broadcasting studios in Relay Park where the television show was being filmed. Our reward was fifteen rand per kid, food and drink for the day as well as the awesome opportunity to appear on television. I loved it and held on to that fifteen rand for all that it was worth, as to ensure that I spend it wisely and let it stretch as far as possible. During the shooting of the show, I was required to appear to attend a garden tea with *The Tubby Giant*, all of this being done whilst being filmed by a camera crew for the next exciting episode. We could not wait for this to air, as this made our school and the few selected children celebrities for a few days. We basked in the glory of having our five minutes of fame.

Living in a neighbourhood like Tranquillity also meant that we had no money for going away on holiday. Year in and year out, we would spend our school holidays at home, keeping busy and playing the way kids did at that age, in the late seventies and early eighties.

So, the one day, during school assembly, a very excited headmaster was bursting to share the joyous news with us.

"Dear scholars. Every year there is an opportunity for scholars to partake in the Holiday Seaside School Breakaway opportunity. This is a sponsorship from a national newspaper that makes it possible for less privileged children to be able to enjoy a Christian holiday at the sea."

This took place during school holidays and was usually for a period of ten days excluding the time that it took to travel to the Breakaway resort. The opportunity to attend was arranged more specifically during summer so that children could experience a seaside holiday in all its splendour. I immediately perked up and listened to the headmaster more earnestly, as I could not believe my ears. A seaside holiday, with the beach and the roaring waves. All expenses paid for. Must be too good to be true.

The headmaster again advised us that children who wanted to go had to volunteer their names for selection after their parents signed a consent and disclaimer form and only children who had never been to the coast before were allowed to volunteer and would be considered. Both Sis and I had obviously never been to the sea before so we jumped at the opportunity and had given our names as volunteers, and astonishingly, both of us were chosen to go at the same time.

On the Tuesday morning we left, Mom, unfortunately, was ill in bed with flu and could not see us off. The neighbour who had a car and with whom Mom arranged then took us to the Fisher Fountain Train and Bus Depot, where we would board a bus with all the other fortunate children selected which would take us to the Holiday Seaside hostel. Although quite early in the morning, the excitement in the air was palpable. We were going to the sea. No wait, we were going on holiday! The bus journey felt like it took an eternity to get to its final destination. We left at the crack of dawn and arrived in Durban at dusk, with the smell of salt and sea in our nostrils. Where is it, where is this azure landscape that we have only seen in pictures and photos and heard about from so many lucky and fortunate enough to have been there before on many occasions and who spoke about it so often? Not being able to see the sea that evening we arrived was a big let-down and disappointment. But then again, this also added to the excitement growing inside of each child, forty-two children from different walks of life, all being able to experience a seaside holiday for the very first time. What a fantastic time we had. For this first time in my life at the age of eleven, I encountered the ocean in real life.

"Close your mouth," a close school friend of mine who also was selected said to me. But, I knew he was just as in awe as I was. As was everyone around us. This simply cannot be true. Blue, azure, and sapphire coloured water wherever you look. Never ending blue, different hues of blue, even at times hinting on green, with waves crashing, ebbing and frothing foam. So delightfully cool. And the beach sand, so warm beneath your feet, slightly bristly, but enjoyable. My feet. On a beach. For the first time in my whole life. One day, when I am big, I thought to myself, I want to live by the sea. I want to hear the roaring of the waves in my ears as I fall asleep and I want to awake with the smell and sound of the magnificence of the sea. Life could not get any better than that, I dreamed.

So for the next ten days, at the Seaside Breakaway resort, we had to follow a fixed routine. Breakfast in the morning at seven o'clock, to be finished by all by nine. Then off to the sea, Bible lessons in the afternoon after lunch, which was between twelve and two, then some playtime, evening assembly, dinner and then bedtime. Every day three special verses from the Bible were selected, and if your name was called during evening assembly, you had to recite one of the three verses off the top of your head, depending on which one was allocated to you to recite from memory. Oh, the anticipation. Never knowing if your name was going to be called, and then which verse would they expect you to recite in front of everyone in the assembly hall. The best thing was to make sure every day that you had all three verses memorised. In addition to this, at the end of ten days, they had a list of thirty well-known verses in the Bible. Boys and girls, who could recite all thirty verses, including the chapter and verse where they reside within the Bible, each received a gift. Sis and I both recited all thirty verses before the end of our vacation, and we received our gifts, dolls for the girls and chess and checkers sets for the boys. Leaving the coastal town of Durban to return to Tranquillity created ambivalence with me, as on the one hand, I terribly missed Mom and wanted to be home with her again, but on the other hand, I was leaving the coast, a dream and some newly made friends behind.

Although Tranquillity was a thoroughfare to other destinations and suburbs, this assured that Tranquillity indeed was close or centre to certain attractions as well. Once a year, the Grand Annual Parade Show would come to town. In those days, it was very close to Fisher Fountain before it relocated to the southern suburbs in later years. And as parking space was limited and probably too expensive, patrons would park their cars alongside the roads that led to the Parade and Show-grounds and walk to the entrance in Fisher Park, which was less than two kilometres away from where they left their vehicles behind. To ensure that everyone had parking and could drive off when they returned from the Parade Show, several children of Tranquillity were masters at directing vehicles and ensuring that everyone had a spot to park in.

"Parking, parking. Parking available over here."

This was the incessant calling from the children alerting patrons on where to park their vehicles. Sis was a skilled master in this and every year when the Parade Show was hosted, she had no problems directing and showing people where to park their cars and received payment in return for helping them but also for watching over their cars. I could never do so, too ashamed to be seen as a poor scoundrel and loathed the idea of people taking pity on me for being poor.

And while Sis was parking cars, I kept a hawk's eye out for Mom, for we were both in for quite a hiding if Mom saw what we did for money.

"We may be poor but we are no beggars," Mom used to say.

But Mom did not understand that we coveted going to the Parade Show. The rides, the attractions, the atmosphere. All of this we wanted to so much to be a part of. So, as we knew there would never be money for us to go and we could never ask Mom, as we already knew what the answer would be, we made a plan of our own. Sis would do her best at parking and watching cars while I would be vigilant and on the lookout for Mom. Should Mom be looking for Sis, she was always with some friend, and I then would warn Sis to lay low while she was waiting for the owner of the car to return. Mom never caught us in the act, and I suspect somehow she never wanted to catch us, as by allowing us this adventure, she silently acquiesced even if she could never vocally and openly approve.

After a few days of parking and watching cars, and being on a stakeout for Mom, we would then count the total earnings. Tragically, despite all this effort, we seldom had enough money for entrance fees for the two of us as well as paying for the rides.

***

Thinking of Tranquillity somehow made me uneasy, and so I stood up from the bed, the rain still pelting the window and the barren winter earth around it. I went into the bathroom and turned on the hot shower. I undressed, stepped into the shower and started taking a long hot shower, hoping to forget, hoping to stop these floodgates of memories that threatened to overwhelm and drown me. Standing in the shower, however, inadvertently my mind returned to Tranquillity again and back to the time when Sis was parking cars for pocket money.

***

This one particular year we heard that there were many new attractions and rides at the Parade Show and this time around despite all Sis' efforts, we again did not have enough money to pay the entrance fees at the Parade Show and still have funds available for all the attractions and rides. But, with all the excitement around the revamped Parade Show, we so desperately wanted to go. So, we heard some kids talking when they returned from the Parade Show, competing with Sis trying to assist with parking the most cars. These boys, full of bravado, boasted about finding a broken fence on the border between the Parade Show and the Freedom Park Tennis Club that allowed them free entrance to the Parade Show-grounds without ever paying any entrance fees, so all their money could be spent on rides and sweets. Not that they would have had enough money for all of this in any case, but somehow they found a way to skip the exorbitant entrance fee and spend their money wisely.

"I don't believe you!" Sis countered the one boy's bravado. "For if there really was a broken fence you would be there every day."

"Don't be silly," the boy responded. "It is no use now if we can get in every day but we have no money for the rides or for food."

Could this be true? Keen to explore this option and to see if there was any truth in their boasting. Sis, me and a family friend of ours went down to the tennis club, and as luck would have it, after searching the perimeter wall and fence for almost an hour, we finally found out that his boasting was true as we managed to locate the broken fence. Voilà! We had access to the Parade Show without paying any entrance fee. Although we entered the premises illegally, this thought never crossed our minds. What joy to save on the entrance fees, what joy to be able to experience it all! So we wandered around, and eventually, as kids always are, we got hungry. The one takeaway restaurant had some sit-down patrons in the shade below and old elm tree and the leftover food not eaten by these patrons was placed on a trolley to be carted away and possibly thrown away. We stared at the food, ogled it more likely as the aroma and the texture of the chicken simply made our mouths water.

"I am hungry," said I to Sis. "And we do not have enough money for food."

"I will make a plan," said Sis.

The next moment, she walked past the trolley and swiped the leftover food. We all made a dash for it and had some great fried chicken leftovers. And felt a little ashamed for snatching the food off the trolley.

"It is not stealing," Sis tried to rationalise and justify between moments of licking off her fingers. "They would have thrown it all away in any case."

"Yes, you must be right." I concurred, enjoying the succulent roast chicken far too much to let our actions deter me.

Something this good, to be thrown away, for whatever reason? I simply could not fathom it. So we did them a favour by enjoying the food that was prepared.

And as we sat there, licking our fingers and enjoying our swiped but delicious meal, unbeknownst to us we were spotted by what we came to believe to be quite a rich lady. Diamond rings on every finger, diamond and ruby necklaces and bangles and bracelets, this lady most certainly had it all. And to us, children from Tranquillity she also seemed poised and stylish. And despite all the stone around her neck and arms and on her fingers, her heart proved to be light, soft and caring.

She slowly walked up to us; cautious as to not scare us off, as we were ready to scatter the moment we smelled trouble. Without referring to what she just witnessed, the lady took fifty rand from her purse and gave it to Sis.

"No, ma'am," Sis said. "Thank you, but we simply cannot accept your money."

"And why is that, young lady?" the lady asked Sis with a twinkle in her eye.

"We were told to never accept gifts from strangers. To not talk to strangers and never take money from strangers," I blurted out.

"Wise words for one so young," the lady opined. "And advice that I most certainly agree with. But look, my children could not make it here today, as they are away studying overseas. And I do know that they would have had fun on all these rides. I kept the money in my purse specifically looking for someone who makes me think of them when they were younger. And the three of you most certainly fall into that category."

I most certainly doubt that the three of us could remind her of her own children. Albeit that Mom always made sure that we were clothed properly, we by no means had any expensive clothing and it was clear that we were impoverished.

"So what would you like us to do with the money, ma'am?" Sis asked. "And what would you expect from us in return?"

"All that I want is for you to have fun," was all she said. I cringed. On the one hand, elated that we had more money for sweets and many rides than what we could ever have dreamt of, but on the other hand, accepting a handout from a stranger. A God sent one but it hurt. What would Mom say? How would Mom feel?

"Do you mind if we talk about it first?" Sis asked the kind lady. She graciously nodded and stood aside.

"What are we going to do?" Sis asked.

"Take the money," our friend suggested.

"It is no different than being paid for parking cars in any case," I said. "As the people know where to park so they are only kind. And this lady is very kind. Think of what we can do with all the money."

"Ok," Sis said. "You go accept the money."

"What? Why me? You are the oldest," I argued.

"No, if you take the money I know you will not tell Mom," Sis said.

"Never. We already took food that does not belong to us, so if I rat on you taking the money, we are in for it in any case for taking the food," I rationalised indignantly.

Best to keep this one to ourselves, we finally decided and agreed upon, after much deliberation, debating and rationalising. Sis, red in the face and looking down the whole time walking towards the lady, managed to remember her manners, gracefully accepted and thanked the lady for the money. We then made a dash for it, leaving the lady behind as we ran off to go and spend the money wisely. The thought of being able to spend all of the money on all the sweets and all the rides that this fifty rand could buy was a dream come true.

"I want to try the Red Rotor ride first!" I squealed in delight. "Then the bumping cars, then the big dipper."

"Let's also go in the haunted house, even do the looping star!" Sis could not keep her excitement out of her voice. "And let's also try for some prizes at the fish pond and gun barrel"

We had an absolute ball of a time, only leaving the Parade Show after seven o'clock that evening chatting and reliving our experiences. We knew very well that Mom would not be concerned, as she knew we were somewhere safe. Perhaps with friends or family members and that it was easy and not very far for us to walk home to from wherever we came from. In those days, life was carefree and extremely simple what with all the other people leaving the Parade Show after their own day of fun and excitement, the area was sure to be bustling with crowds and people returning from having a joyful day.

***

Having etched up this memory again, I felt my cheeks burning again and was reminded of the shame we felt in receiving a hand out from a stranger, albeit that we were elated and overjoyed with the prospect of having money. Wherever this lady is today, I believe that the Lord has had His hand on her the whole time, for she cared about us as if we were her own. It does not take the feeling of utter desolation away, nor does it reduce the humiliation at all. I told myself this was enough of memory lane for one day. I looked at my cell phone, but there was no WhatsApp message, no BBM, no one interested in talking to me on this cold and rainy winter's day. Alone with only my memories, I switched on the air conditioner in the upstairs lounge to heat up the room, took a book and a blanket and went to lie down in the bay window, staring out at the raindrops running like tears down the window. Reluctantly, but unable to concentrate on the book I was trying to read, I went back to continue my stroll down Tranquillity Lane. And with a start, as I thought of strolling down Tranquillity Lane, I remembered the bus lane that ran through Tranquillity...

***

Tranquillity was also the hub that connected several other western suburbs to the main centre of town, and the bus service ran through Tranquillity on a regular bus schedule. We had five different bus stops that one could embark on when journeying into the centre of town, and four to disembark from when coming from central town. Living in Tranquillity with its hustle and bustle albeit all surrounded by poverty, I spent my days as a child talking to the Lord, as the Lord was the best friend I ever had, growing up in poverty. The Lord was a patient listener and I could take anything and everything I had to the Lord. And I firmly believed, and still believe, that the Lord's presence is always in one's life. I remember the day after I received that very important call that I was successful in getting a job. Sis then was working for five years already and she promised to buy me a few outfits for work. So the one Saturday Sis went to work, we arranged that I would catch a bus into town, meet her at a clothing store around eleven o'clock, and we would go on a shopping spree. Gleeful. New clothes to look spick and span on my first day! I planned to take the half past ten bus into town, as it was a mere twenty minutes to the stop where I needed to get off. But on this particular Saturday, there simply was no bus.

I waited and waited, and started getting impatient, for I was afraid that Sis would think that I was not able to meet her, and she would return home. By half past eleven, there was still no bus, and I was totally conflicted. I started arguing with the Lord, blaming the Lord for delaying the bus, blaming the Lord for not being there for me when I needed him the most. I even accused the Lord of being vindictive. I was in two minds. Should I go or should I stay? When the bus finally arrived at a quarter to twelve, I decided to hop on. The bus was decidedly empty despite the delay in schedule and all the way, I was fighting with the Lord. When I finally disembarked from the bus at the stop that would take me to the clothing store, I was quite worked up and hoped that Sis would be waiting for me. As I crossed the promenade on my way to the clothing store, I spotted Sis standing waiting for me. Without looking, being so elated that she did not decide to get on a bus and returned home, more so that I was able to get a new set of clothes, I started to run to Sis, who was on the opposite side of the road. Oblivious to everything around me, not looking at traffic or heeding any traffic lights, I simply ran towards Sis. The next moment, Sis screamed at the top of her lungs, and I managed to realise that it was to warn me of impending danger. But too late. As I turned I saw a car coming straight at me, and I knew that there was simply no way to get out of its way. As the car hit my legs, I pressed my arms on the hood of the car and I cartwheeled right over the car and landed on my feet, able to run across the street without any further incident. Sis all but collapsed.

"Oh, dear Lord! Are you okay?" Sis asked in tears.

"I am fine, quite shaken, look at my hands. My legs also feel a bit stiff but that is all."

"You were really very lucky! Why did you not look out for any traffic? This is the centre of town, for heaven's sake. I almost thought you were going to be killed. How did you do that?"

"Only God will know," was all that I was able to muster.

And I knew immediately, that this was the Lord talking to me. It was the Lord's way of making me realise how unfair I was making me reconfirm the Lord's presence in my life. So I got a lot more than I bargained for on that day. Sis and I returned to Tranquillity, with a lot of new clothes for me, but also with the knowledge that one never mocks the Lord. The Lord will always be there for one, even in a place like Tranquillity, or perhaps especially in a place like it.

Tranquillity. Over the years, we were forced to move house a few times in Tranquillity. The first time we moved, we were forced by the local municipality to look for another place to stay as they planned to demolish our house in Serene Street. We then went to stay in a semi-detached house in Still Street that belonged to one of my cousins. He rented the house to us for eleven rand a month. This house was a huge improvement on the previous house in Serene Street. The house had a green exterior, and it had two separate bedrooms, and a bathroom, with a bath and toilet all inside the house! Granted, still no geyser and no hot water, but oh, the joy to be bathing in an actual bath and no longer washing up in a bucket and to do away with that dreaded chamber pot finally. Ecstasy!

A few years later, we moved again, from Still Street to Calm Street. This was pure luxury. Now our house consisted of three bedrooms, hot water, bath and toilet all inside. What more could one ask for in life? Sheer bliss. At this time, Sis and I both were working, so we managed to rent this up-scaled luxurious property (as luxurious as it could get in Tranquillity). So, for the first time in my life, I finally experienced what it was to have hot running water in a bathroom. We stayed there for a year when the owner was forced to sell due to financial difficulty. Albeit that this was in comparison to what we were used to a grand house to stay in, we simply could not afford to buy this house, so we moved back to Still Street again, however, to a different house that became available to us to rent. With us now being able to be slightly fussier, this time around we would not settle for less than what we had and got used to in Calm Street.

"We have seen a house that we like," said Mom to me one evening when I returned from tutoring some friends' children for extra cash, which I did every evening after work. I had to repay my study debt and pay towards my own living expenses and needed what extra income I could get to assist me with my responsibilities.

"It is in Composed Street and belongs to Uncle Mac. The house is in the market and has everything we already have and more – it includes a pool as well. The house is going for far less than what Mr Robertson was asking."

Sis looked at me and said, "I think we should make an offer and try to buy the house".

We did our sums and realised that if we bought Uncle Mac's property at the price that Uncle Mac wanted, we would only be paying slightly more than what we were paying currently for renting the house we lived in. Without thinking or even knowing what the property looked like, I agreed that it was the right thing to do to apply for a bond, as it was also about time that we stopped paying off other people's mortgages. The bond was approved and Sis and I bought the property together. Our own home. Our very own house. We are now no longer the low poor class people we once were. Poor class, we perhaps were, but honest. We were by no means rich now, we were not even middle class yet, but we now owned property. It was a start. Enchanting.

We stayed in Composed Street for three years, but due to neighbours across the street running a shebeen (a place where alcohol was sold illegally), Sis could not stand the tension of people accessing these premises all the time and the police raiding the premises at odd hours in the early mornings. Sis was more in tears and hated what life in Composed Street became. We had to always be on the lookout as not the best of customers frequented the illegal shebeen, so we were potential targets for muggings and robberies the whole time. So one night we sat down as a family and decided that the best thing for us was to move. This time around out of Tranquillity completely, as Sis and I simply no longer were happy in Tranquillity. It took quite some convincing to do with Mom, as she stayed there all her life, and despite the fact that urban decay was affecting Tranquillity, this was in her blood. Mom only gave in when we assured her that we would drop her off in the mornings on our way to work and pick her up each evening after work, as long as she cleared this with her friends and my aunt and them who were still making a living in Tranquillity. This Mom did, and it became a standard routine for several years.

***

Snugly under a blanket with the air conditioner spraying its hot waves all over the upstairs lounge, I reflected that after spending my entire childhood and teenage years in Tranquillity, we finally kicked the dust off our feet and left Tranquillity behind just before I turned twenty-five. Although Tranquillity had a lot to do with who I am today,

I never once looked back and felt that I missed the suburb or neighbourhood at all. I learned many lessons, good and bad, had many heartaches and sadness. But, Tranquillity was no longer a part of me and no longer where I wanted to be. It was time to leave poverty behind and this was the first step in doing so. I knew very little tranquillity living there, and had faith that the start of a new life in a new suburb would be the origin of living a better life and for better things to come our way. I also realised that the place does indeed make the man, that I could have grown up anywhere else and would possibly have been a different person.

Looking at the dark clouds with the continuous rain, I briefly wondered who and what I would have been. I realised with a start that even if things could have been different, I would have preferred to be who I was right then. That poverty was a chalice that I could never carry with pride, that as a result of poverty I had an urge to succeed and be the best in what I did. And that I did not want to trade for the world. For the first time in almost four decades, I did not abhor thinking of being poor. That is a start in the right direction. The hole in my soul created by poverty will always be there, but it has driven me to make a promise that we as a family will never again go to bed without food, that we will never want for anything in life again. My aim never was and still is not to be rich; my aim is to be comfortable. And that was the lesson the hole of poverty taught me.

Peckish, I went down the stairs into the kitchen and ate some breakfast, cereal with raisins and milk. Walking up the stairs back to the comfort of my blanket, I started to think of survival. How we managed to get by as a family remembering with fondness and more than a touch of melancholy.

35

FAFI

Some of my earliest childhood memories of survival that threatened to engulf me on this cold and desolate rainy winter's day. It inevitably reminded me of a father, Mom, Sis and a few family members and friends; who all in some way formed me or contributed towards my growth in some significant way (not all of them, but most of them anyway).

Growing up in poverty was never going to be easy, one learned from a very early age that one could never have what others had, that you would always be and feel inferior to those who had and it was best to as far as possible avoid them like the plague. Even Tranquillity had its own class system, and we fell smack in the lowest class of it all. Low class does not mean common, as we most certainly were not a common family. We had a great upbringing in terms of discipline but we would never be able to leave the trail of poverty behind. With a father loving the bottle more than grafting and doing an honest day's labour, and one who was at work less than being off work, we as a family had no choice but to rely on a mother who fended for her children with all she had in her. A mother so protective of her whelps that she as far as possible tried to make sure that her whelps will not go without food or clothes, albeit a meagre meal and some bargain store or second hand clothing purchased.

***

"Mom, why is it that you never help us with our home-work?" I asked Mom one day.

"There is no need to help you and Sis. You know what is required from you and I do not need to check up on you," Mom said.

"How was school in Mom's days?" I would probe.

"I never enjoyed it much," Mom said.

Mom would then tell us the story of her youth. How Mom never had a proper education and left school in which today is known as grade eight but in those days it was called standard six. As Mom simply could not adjust to learning and doing school-work, at a young age she left school and went to work for a few years at the local post office.

"It was a way to make money and a means to help Grandma and Grandpa as well, as they most certainly did not have it great in life."

"So what did you do at the post office? Did you work with stamps and letters?"

"No, we were not customer facing," Mom would answer me. "We were back office staff that had to clean the telephones after they were repaired and due to be delivered to the next household. It was boring but it provided an income."

At the tender age of eighteen, Mom met my father, resigned from her job, got married at the age of nineteen and never found work again due to her lack of proper scholastic education. However, Mom was a stalwart and she found a way to provide for her offspring. She did this by running an illegal local gambling game called Fafi (pronounced fah-fee).

Fafi. A lifesaver and a God send. A means of providing income. A gambling game, a means of survival. The way the game works is that you select any number from one to thirty-six and you place a bet on that number. The numbers each had a different meaning ascribed to it and usually, if one had a dream and could remember some remnants of that fast-fading dream, it invariably could be translated into one or more of these thirty-six numbers, and you would place your bet on these numbers. Each number also was associated with another number, its own partner number, so when you played the one number it was recommended to also play and bet on the partner number as well, as the Fafi game works better when you placed your bets on pairs. During those years, you could play from as little as five cents and as much as one hundred rand, which was the maximum bet. So, if one person wanted to bet one hundred rand, no other person could play that number for that day. But, one hundred rand was a lot of money in those days, so you most certainly had to believe in your dream to take such a huge risk. The odds were always twelve to one, so for betting five cents, if your number was drawn, you then would get sixty cents. In the late seventies and early to late eighties, this was quite a lot of money for a kid. Children were not allowed to place bets, but as Mom was running the game, she did not mind to place bets on my behalf. If I won, she would deduct the money that I played from my winnings, and if I lost, Mom would stand good for it. The gambling game was against the law, but for a mother feeding and clothing her children, this was not a deterrent. The people playing this game are called punters. And by Jove, Mom had many punters. There were times that they queued right into our backyard in order for them to come and place their bets. In fact, my mom was known as the Fafi Queen in Tranquillity, and her punters were from all ethnic groups, blacks, whites, Indian and coloureds. My mother knew no racial lines and did not care about these, she saw no colour, as she believed all people were equal, and hence had no problem with who her punters were.

Mom was not the only one running the game, there were two other runners as well, the one running in the evening and the other running over weekends. The system worked well between the runners as well.

When playing the game of Fafi, which provided a selection of thirty-six numbers preferably played with partners, punters would come and bet on a number, and Mom would then write and record their numbers in a book, together with the amount they had placed as a bet on each number. This Mom then re-recorded on another separate page, the page that kept track of the total amount of money that was being placed as a bet on a number, as she could never allow more than one hundred rand at a time per number. Some punters had a list of their own numbers, others came to my Mom and played and placed bets, and Mom then would record their numbers and then also write it down for them on a piece of paper to ensure that there is always a record of the punting that took place. Each record was marked in a special way by Mom to enable Mom to identify whether the numbers, in fact, were played or punted on that specific day. After all, you do not want a punter to have an old record coming to claim winnings that were not for that day!

At or just about after one o'clock in the afternoon, my mother then would take a copy of the recording, and hand this to the banker for the game of Fafi, who was of Chinese descendant. The Chinese man always pre-decided what number is going to be drawn. This is done during an exchange, as he does not know how many punters punted the specific number that he exchanged with my mother when she takes a copy of the full record to him and he hands her a single number between one and thirty-six on a small piece of paper. This then would be the winning number! For each number, there was a hand signal that was given, so that every punter knew immediately what number was drawn and became the winning number. Some punters left in disgust, that dream of theirs not realising any income. Others smiled hugely as they won and still others regretted not betting more money on the winning number. But, they would all be back the next day; the faithful and converted, as the game that Mom was the runner for was on a daily basis, weekdays only.

All of this takes place and was made possible with the Chinese man taking the risk on the payout, as he was the banker. However, if the daily earnings were greater than the payout and commission, the latter paid to Mom; the Chinese man pocketed the net result. His name was Tommy, and for many years, he and my mother had this system going. They did the exchange covertly, like a special SWAT unit; always on the lookout for the cops as in those days as gambling was against the law, one faced hefty fines and even imprisonment if one was caught.

Fafi and the income derived from it was the only source of income that kept us as a family alive, clothed and ensured that we had a roof over our heads during our early childhood to early adult years. On good days, Mom would pocket anything between thirty and fifty rand and on bad days anything between ten and thirty rand. Mom used this money to buy groceries, pay for other expenses, saved some money for Christmas presents and clothing and used the rest for some other special occasions.

On one of these occasions, Mom managed to save for more than two years and finally on one special day Mom used these savings as a down payment on a Blaupunkt television set.

During the day, Mom called us together as a family. "I have a very nice surprise in store for us as a family. I will be showing you this surprise sometime this afternoon, so please be at home by five."

"What is it, Mom?" I cried out in ecstasy. The suspense was too intense. "When are we getting it? Will it be here at five or are we going to wait? Is it something for each of us or one thing we all are going to share? Please, Mom, tell us, whatever it may be?"

But, Mom was savouring and enjoying this moment far too much to let it be spoilt. Later that afternoon, just after five, here came Mom and two employees from Purcell's, the local Jewish furniture store, carrying a huge cardboard box. What was inside it, we could not guess as the cardboard box was all covered in bubble wrap on the outside as well. When the box was finally opened, to our surprise and delight, Mom had bought a television set. A TV! Wow! We had our very own TV. Surely, we cannot be that poor, I thought to myself, if we now also have a TV. Not that I fully understood what TV was, as I only heard that people had television sets, but never managed to see what the fuss was all about as the people who had television sets most certainly were not mingling with us. Nonetheless, we now had our very own.

Mom very promptly rearranged the lounge so that we had a stand for the TV. She switched it on. And for several minutes we all watched in awe, this colourful globe, which in fact was the signal of the South African Broadcasting Corporation (as in those days, 24-hour television was unheard of). I started to feel uncomfortable. What was all the fuss about?

"Stop fidgeting, my son. Wait and see," Mom said as if she could read my mind.

And at six that evening, the news started showing, and now we were all in awe. News, right here in our own lounge. First-hand. The TV talks and tells you things. And shows you pictures. Moving pictures! Amazing. And this was ours. All bought with Fafi money!

During particular good Fafi stretches, which were not that often as Tranquillity by no means had folk who simply could bet recklessly, punters were betting high amounts on many numbers, Mom would have quite a commission saved up. Every now and then, we were fortunate to go on a Saturday morning to buy groceries in bulk from a grocery store in the far western suburb of Brighton. Mom, Sis and I would walk the more than three kilometres to the grocery store, do the shopping and with plastic bags of goodies, walked the same route back home again, come sunshine or rain. The plastic bags would eat into our hands but *hi ho hi ho* it's on the way to home we go, knowing very well that we would have better than usual food for the next few weeks. And we didn't mind that we did not have enough money for public transport. We would have gladly walked the distance every Saturday if it meant that we had food in our cupboards and meat in our fridge.

Mom loved it. She lived for her children, and for Fafi, as it was a means that provided her purpose. As this was a lifeline for her to provide, but also a way for her I think to show that albeit that scholastically she did not perform, there was nothing wrong with her mind. After all, she worked with figures and money and could calculate winnings in a flash. And, despite the danger and risk of being caught, she continued doing it.

One sunny afternoon during school holidays, I came home from the local swimming pool, which was situated on Blissful Street, and Mom was still busy taking bets from her punters. The next moment, two policemen came barging in from the back porch, running into our house, confiscated the gambling money, searched the house for every penny they could find, including Mom's savings and arrested Mom on the spot. Punters scattered all over the show disappearing frightened that they may be arrested for supporting the game!

"Get hold of Tommy!" Mom managed to cry out and instruct me, pale as a ghost, as she knew that despite her quagmire, Tommy would post the bail money if so required.

Embarrassed and very scared, Mom was hurled into the back of a police van like a common criminal and taken to the nearest police station, which was situated in Brighton. Fortunately, Mom was saved the embarrassment of being handcuffed before being thrown into the vehicle.

Scared witless, I ran to one of the usual exchange points, knowing which one to choose for this specific week, wiping tears from my eyes, which stung like crazy.

"Please, God," I prayed. "Don't let them lock her away. Please, please, please God!"

And then I saw Tommy's car.

"Uncle Tommy," I heaved. "My mom has just been arrested!"

Tommy also went a shade of pale, but immediately took charge of the situation, as he knew what needed to be done.

"Calm down, boy," he said to me. "I will go and make sure your mom is released as soon as possible."

And he did. He posted bail money of one hundred and fifty rand and my mother was released. She had quite a shock to her system, and also was told that she had to appear in court in a fortnight. This troubled my mom, but not enough for her to give up on Fafi, as she knew without the money we would not survive. So for the next couple of days, the punters were not allowed on our premises, Mom would meet them on the street, take their numbers and money, and go back home and place their bets. This was done without Mom discussing it with the punters. Instinctively, they simply knew that Mom would come to them and allow them to place their bets. Mom knew that our house was being watched, so she only returned home once or twice during this time, never to let on that she was still running the gambling game. She risked everything to make living a reality for us all.

Two weeks later, my mother went to court. She was as nervous as hell and asked a friend of hers to accompany her. She later related the story to me as to what happened on that day.

"I arrived at the court at eight in the morning," said Mom, "far too afraid to be late and sent to jail for contempt of court. I sat on a wooden hard uncomfortable bench outside courtroom number 6. I had to wait for my name to be called, all the time talking to Aunt Mary.

"Around one in the afternoon a man all dressed in a uniform opened the court doors and my name was finally called. As I walked into the courtroom on wobbly legs and feet of jelly, I nearly fainted. The most fearsome looking judge sat on the bench and was scowling down at me."

Tommy, Mom mentioned, also arranged for a lawyer to be present in court, ready to pay whatever fine was imposed on my mother. If a fine was imposed, and not imprisonment!

When the judged asked my mother how she was pleading. "Fafi, your Honour" was her answer. The judge had little patience and roared from the bench, "How do you plead, not what gambling game you were running!"

My mother winced and in a small voice answered, "My apologies your honour. Could you please repeat that?"

This just seemed to antagonise him more, but in the end, she managed to plead guilty to the charge. She was found guilty on a misdemeanour charge and was to pay an admission of guilt fine of three hundred rand, and as one hundred and fifty rand was already posted for bail, Tommy's lawyer paid the remaining balance. Free.

"Thank you, Lord," I silently whispered a prayer when Mom arrived at home later that afternoon.

Although all my primary school friends knew Mom as the Fafi Queen, as our primary school was right there in our neighbourhood, this secret was kept from my high school friends, who barring two, never even knew where I lived but even they never knew what Mom did for a living. Poverty had such a stigma for me. I hated it and everything that was associated with it. School fees could not be paid, and each year I had to take a letter to the principal, requesting that I be exempted from paying school fees, as we simply could not make all ends meet if we still had to pay school fees as well out of the Fafi winnings.

Sis, on the other hand, it seemed, had no problem letting people know that we were poor. On a few occasions, the high school she went to sent some parcels to our home, especially when times were tough and rough and Mom could not meet all the financial demands placed on her to run a household and having two children in high school. By this time, my father had passed away, and there was no on-off income other than the Fafi gambling commission that my mother earned and the occasional winnings when she herself placed some bets on some winning numbers.

Then sadly and unexpectedly, Tommy passed away. His family was not interested in pursuing the gambling game and hence we stared the reality in the face of having no income at all. Mom continued to search for a potential gambling partner, but after a while started getting agitated and concerned that she was not going to be successful soon. Her savings for Christmas presents and clothes had to be used to ensure that we had food on the table and eventually her savings started to run dry as well. Mom had to make a plan, and she was like a caged animal. Mustering all the courage she had she knew she had to go and request a temporary allowance from my cousin, until such time that she managed to start the gambling game again.

"Richard. Today I stand before you hat in hand. I am ashamed that I need to ask you for help, but I cannot see my children go without food. I am not worried about me. I am worried for my little ones. They need to be taken care of. I have no doubt that I will be running Fafi again soon. But, until such time, could I please ask you for some money on a weekly basis, only from week to week as I have no doubt that Fafi will begin soon again. Please have mercy on us. I know you have your own expenses and life to lead, but just this one time, please favour us with your kindness. I will repay you each cent once I start running Fafi again. I will keep a record of all the times you assisted us. Please, I beg of you," Mom pleaded with and promised him.

"I will lend you twenty rand a week. Every Wednesday you will come and collect until such time that you have started Fafi again. Then we will discuss the repayment options."

With that agreement to pay us twenty rand a week allowance until such time that my mother had started her gambling business again, he took out two ten rand notes and handed these to Mom. Mom had tears in her eyes, humiliated yet humbled and thankful for this gesture.

That was not an easy time. In fact, it was a very hard time for us as a family. Some nights we went to bed without having any food as the money could only be stretched that far. Mom simply could not muster the courage to ask for more money. Somehow, Mom always felt humiliated when she went to collect the money. At times Richard kept Mom waiting for the money, perhaps only giving it to her the following day. I heard my mother praying for an outcome night after night and I saw my mother crying herself to sleep. But, her faith never faltered, not once.

One evening, hungry again with no food, we had some spaghetti in the cupboard. I boiled the spaghetti and had some tomato sauce sachets that I used to give the spaghetti some flavour. An acquaintance of my mother happened to come by and noticed what I was eating. She then immediately offered that we could have lunch at her place every day, and she would let her domestic servant know that she should be serving lunch to us as well. This turned out to be an empty promise. When we arrived for lunch the first day, Mom had to swallow all her pride and take us to the acquaintance's home, the domestic servant who opened the door had no knowledge of it and mentioned that she would speak to the madam and we should come back the next day. And the next day, the door was not opened. Despite our knocking and calling, the door was never opened. Closed. Just like an empty promise from a hardened heart. We never knew the reason for a promise made not being honoured, perhaps the lady also realised that she only had enough for her and her own family and regretted her spontaneous reaction, her impulsive reaction to our dire situation. But, Mom never spoke about this incident again, and the acquaintance never referred to it again. As if it never happened.

But, through all this humiliation and suffering, yet my mother persevered. Finally, she managed to find a new gambling partner. How she did this, I will never know, as Mom never owned a car, could not drive and had no money for public transport. But, she found a gambling banking partner and started the game all over again. The first thing she did once she had enough money saved was to repay her debt to my cousin in terms of the weekly allowance and stipend paid to us whilst my mother was searching for a gambling partner.

This new partner, who went by the name of Wong, had a different way of exchanging the number and the records. Wong was afraid of being caught by the police, so he did not want to do the exchange from his car. He designed a device that was in the form of a metal box. The metal box had a lock at the top, which could only be opened by Wong himself. The way it worked was that Wong would insert the winning number in the shift lock itself. So when the lock is moved to lock position, a piece of paper containing the winning number is released and the metal box locked and closed. Hence, if the lock is shifted into lock position, the metal box would be locked from the inside, where the record of the betting was to be inserted. This worked quite well. Mom would insert the betting records, close the lid, move the shift lock to lock position, and out came the winning number for the day. Wong then at different times on different days would collect the box, remove the betting records and insert a new winning number for the following day.

This went on for several years. One day, on school holidays again, I helped Mom with the betting, as I was quite familiar with the game of Fafi and had no problem assisting Mom when needed. Sis, on the other hand, was never at home during Fafi time, as she was always afraid of being caught. On this particular day, it was a very busy day, payday for many punters and therefore many punters were punting and betting their winning numbers.

"Sandra, for luck, you can draw the winning number today," Mom said to one of her friends, pointing to the metal box.

In her haste to do so, and to my horror, Sandra took the metal container and closed the box without inserting the exchange betting record. The winning number was revealed, and the box was locked with the recording of the day still in Mom's hand.

"Oh, hell, I am sorry!" Sandra cried out. "What are we going to do now?"

In a flash, I could see that Wong would accuse us of being dishonest and that he would no longer allow my mother to be his gambling partner. With tears in my eyes, fear in my heart, and a forlorn feeling of utter despair, I made a dash for it and ran out of the house. I ran and ran and ran until I could no longer run, all the way crying and praying for an outcome, for us to survive this, as I simply did not want to go hungry again. What are we going to do? We most certainly cannot tell Wong this, as he would not believe our story, doesn't matter how credible the explanation or how true it was. But we needed to find a way around this quandary. And, fast.

The Lord smiled upon us. While racking my brain to find a solution, it was as if it was laid out in front of me. When I returned home, Mom was dumbfounded, no one had been paid their winnings yet, as Mom did not want to jeopardise the game. Mom believed that she needed to wait for Wong and show him that we did not pay out any of the punters and that we should declare the day as stale. But, Mom was still concerned, and many of the punters who would have been winners on this day were not happy with this approach.

"I know what we need to do," I said to Mom. "We have to find a way of inserting the betting record into the metal box without Wong noticing anything," I whispered to Mom.

"Please ask the punters to wait outside."

I then took the metal container and the betting record, and I folded it and slowly tried to insert it on the side of the metal container. There was just enough room on the groove on the side to actually make this work! When the betting record was inside the metal container through the groove, I started to shake the box and all that I could do was hope and pray that the piece of paper would have moved and settled in the box like every other day.

That evening, when Wong came and opened the metal container, anxiously and with bated breath Mom and I stared at him, hoping and praying that nothing was amiss. When Wong opened the container, the paper was standing upright against the edge. Wong did not think anything about it and possibly thought it was the way the record was inserted in the metal box. We all afterwards sighed a huge sigh of relief that all was well. Our income was secured, which was under threat by something as simple as an honest mistake!

Later on, when I recounted my flight from the house, running and crying, and that all I could think of was to make a run for it, Mom howled with laughter, more a sense of relief that this specific day was not the day that we will go hungry again.

49

And so Mom continued to risk her freedom to be in a position to feed and provide for us, up to the point that Sis finished school and started working (she is two years older than me), and I finished high school and went on to university. I took out a student loan, and four years later graduated from university and I started looking for work. During all this time, Sis was a source of income, and with her help, I managed to get to university, be dressed and fed, and Mom continued Fafi for the love of it, and less for the need of it.

***

Thinking of Mom and her fondness for Fafi, I couldn't help but smile, albeit with sadness, at the lengths that Mom went to in order for us to have food on the table. Many a night we did go hungry, as the winnings were not always enough to ensure that we as a family enjoyed a proper meal. Even when it was no longer necessary for Mom to run the game, she continued, as somehow this was something that she clung to. Until there was no longer a need for it as her punters moved on to different games, providing different odds and were deemed to be above board.

I resented my dream, and more so wished that I hadn't heard those words in the song, as on that Saturday morning, the floodgates were opened. And somehow, I could not seem to be able to close these floodgates, it was as if a white squall has broken loose on my sea of memories, flooding my emotions. It was as if my soul had a hunger to devour these memories, to relive them again, to make me see what has caused so many hurtful blows to it. Perhaps it was to still a deeply ingrained hunger for tranquillity and acceptance.

And, try as I might, I could not stop remembering. How hunger and fear and humiliation were all such a big part of my life, causing blows to my soul, silently yet effectively punching holes into my soul…

FOOD AND HUNGER

Mom was a fantastic cook (no baking though), and she passed her love of Indian curry dishes and strong, spicy food on to Sis and me. Mom taught Sis how to cook from an early age, and also taught me how to cook so that anyone at any time could be called upon to make food. Mom loved her afternoon naps and if we were hungry enough, we would start preparing food early. This all depended on how much food we had and how great a week Mom had with her commission. I was always hungry and sometimes could not wait for the food to finish cooking.

"Mom, could I please have some food, I am starving?"

"The food is not ready yet, it is going to be a while still."

"I don't mind, just some rice please Mom with some gravy?" I would beg, convinced that I was about to starve to death.

Mom then would give me some half-cooked rice in a cup and added the curry gravy to this. Absolutely manna from heaven. This got me out of her hair until the food was finally ready and could be served. Mom would only shake her head in wonderment in how I was able to eat hard half-raw rice and then add a curry flavour to it all!

Then there were days that we did not have food in abundance. On those days, we would have bread, with either pilchards in tomato sauce or pilchards in chilli sauce. On other occasions, we would have canned beans in tomato sauce, or canned spaghetti in tomato sauce, as this was all that we could afford to eat and to still this constant gnawing hunger.

One day my mother unexpectedly received guests, and they were all hungry. So they all chipped in and bought some minced meat and eggs, and made a mixture of eggs and minced meat. This became a meal that we would have many times in future when times were tough, as it was a most affordable meal. To this day, I abhor scrambled eggs with mince, any canned dish in tomato sauce and any sardines or pilchards.

And more often than not, there was not enough money to also provide us with lunch for school, as Mom had to pay the monthly rental on the house, the utilities. Ensuring too that we had as close to a decent meal in the evening, as well as paying for public transport to get Sis and me to our respective high schools, which were both located outside of Tranquillity. To this day I do not know what Sis did at school, but I always pretended to not be hungry, only to gladly albeit supposedly reluctantly accept the sandwich offered to me from time to time by my school friends. Somehow, I suspect they knew, but even in childhood or more like adolescence, they knew the fine line between simply asking and actually embarrassing me about me never bringing any lunch to school, never spending any money at the tuck shop and never showing that I was hungry. So I was taken care of in my own way by the few close school friends who never minded sharing their lunch meals with me. And I never asked. Not once. But when they offered, I almost always accepted, jokingly teasing them that I was watching their dietary intake. And due to not having breakfast either, if at times my stomach would rumble too loudly in class before lunch break, I would ask to go to the bathroom and drink a lot of water to still my gnawing hunger and protesting tummy.

One evening, Mom, Sis and I went to a friend's house, as my father was on the binge again and we had no money for food. We walked the few blocks to the friend's house, simply to get away from it all. The smell of alcohol, the tempers that went with it and the flurry of friends all too eager to share a drop with my father. A father who was too eager to share and have rowdy yet needy friends around him. And who made life intolerable more often than not.

"I cannot take this much longer," Mom told her friend. "His drinking is getting worse. He now even uses the money that we need for food. I have to hide money to make sure that we eat every evening."

"Why don't you just leave him?" the friend asked Mom.

"Where will he go to?" Mom asked her. "If I leave him, he will surely die. He is the father of my children. But he is no longer the man I married."

"Would you like to have something to eat?" the friend asked Mom. "I have just finished cooking so we are ready to have supper."

"No, thank you," Mom said. "My timing is off. I will come visit you at some other time."

"Don't be foolish," the friend said to Mom. "I have more than enough food for all of us. I can see that your kids are hungry. That is what friends are for."

Mom's friend then starting placing the food on the table, and I realised that she indeed had plenty of food. Odd-looking meat was in a bowl, but the aroma was simply overwhelming. My mouth was watering and I had to swallow the saliva a few times. Whatever smelt so appetising could only be a culinary feast!

"What would you like to eat?" Mom's friend asked me. As I was quite shy, I pointed to the funny looking meat on the plate. The next moment, my hand stung as Mom slapped my hand away.

"It is rude to point at food!" Mom scolded me.

Geez, Mom, I thought to myself, if I knew what the meat was called I would have asked for it. But I was too embarrassed to say anything further, and so Mom's friend dished up for us and filled our plates with everything that was on offer. Meat, vegetables, hot bread and potatoes. A culinary feast fit for a king. Mom was very grateful, and we spent a wonderful evening at Mom's friend, where after we had to return home, as Mom was afraid that my father would start looking for her. Not finding her would lead to an argument, and this would continue into the early hours of the morning.

"Mom," I said. "Why are we poor?"

"It is the Lord's will," Mom retorted.

"But why us, Mom?"

"We do not question the ways of the Lord. Accept your fate and make the best of it."

"Mom, I am sorry if I embarrassed you this evening. I did not know the meat and therefore could not ask for it."

"You could have merely said that you would like a piece of meat. You did not need to point at the food. No one should ever think that my kids were not brought up having good manners."

"What meat was it, Mom?" I wanted to know.

"Liver, fried with onions." Mom said.

When we arrived home, thankfully the fair-weathered friends who had not left were all passed out, inebriated and as drunk as skunks. That included my father, so at least we had the prospects of having a relatively quiet peaceful evening of sleep.

Poverty and hunger most certainly left its indelible mark on me. Poverty I know now is nothing to be ashamed of, as this has moulded me and made me into the person whom I am today. But the poverty, hunger and humiliation holes in my soul were created as a result of a mother who risked her very freedom to provide food and shelter for her beloved children. Poverty was always associated with risk, with fear and with knowing what we did was against the law. But we had to find some means of surviving, and we did.

Poverty also created shame. And the shame caused the poverty hole to widen. Ashamed that I had to go to the principal and request exemption from paying school fees. Ashamed that we did not have money for any fun, entertainment or even movies. Ashamed that we could not afford new clothes. Ashamed that we never had money to go on holiday. Ashamed that my sister's school at times would bring us food parcels. Ashamed, ashamed, ashamed.

Sis, however, embraced and accepted the fact that this was made out to be our lot in life. I recoiled from it. I made a solemn promise to myself the first night I went hungry without food, that the day that I start to work, my mother, my sister and I will never go hungry again. We may not be rich, but we will have enough food so that we are never reminded of the times where food was a luxury we could not afford. And when I started working, this promise I fulfilled. Slowly, I noticed a change in the hole that was created by poverty. The hole that was so wide due to a mother's fight for survival, children's hunger, apathy from friends and family members and a need to have enough in life started to be filled by living the promise I made. Seeing a mother no longer desperately trying to feed her cubs, a sister trying to financially support a family. This was a combined effort and made a huge difference to us all. Although the hole will never be filled completely, I take comfort in the fact that with the Lord's help, I managed to make good on a promise I made to myself, and to my family.

So these holes that once were canyon wide have narrowed to a small ravine over the years, but remain some of the first holes in my soul. How big can a soul be and how many holes can it take before a soul is destroyed? The holes of poverty, humiliation and hunger however now are no longer the biggest, but will always remain the first holes that punctured, beaten and weathered my soul.

2

THE HOLE OF REJECTION

Looking out the window, the rain still falling, the sky an ominous grey, my mood matched the clouds. I was swept away by the current of emotions and memories, all because of a stupid dream, I told myself. Why the sudden need to reminisce, to relive these moments caught in the moments of time. I was dumbfounded, but the more I tried to divert my attention, or to avoid thinking about the past, the more the floodgates opened and I was carried away by a strong current of memories and emotions. Even switching on the television, I would find something that would remind me of an incident in the past. I finally relented, allowed myself to have the memories wash over me, and allowed the tides of time to ebb and flow in my memory banks. And involuntarily I washed ashore an isle of memories of my father...

A FATHER'S HATRED

I was brought onto this earth and into this world, a little more than four decades ago, born not in a hospital but actually in our own house as Mom's time came far too soon and caught her unawares. Mom's labour was a painful experience, and when I finally made my appearance in this life, my father looked at me and immediately made up his mind to never accept or love me. Mom would relay to me that my father one day in drunken stupor slapped my mother on her tummy during her pregnancy, and today I bear the birthmark on my back to prove it. Coincidence perhaps, but for me reality. A reality of being rejected at birth or even perhaps before birth by my own father. Was it because one more mouth needed to be fed? Was it because it meant less time with Mom? I will never know the answer to this. But I do know that this became hole number two, the hole of rejection.

Growing up with a father who loved the bottle more than his family was always going to be challenging, therefore, staying away from my father at all costs made life and living more bearable. Living out fantasies mostly on my own and only sometimes playing with a few relatives became my ultimate reality. By steering clear from my father, I grew very close to Mom and Sis, both who protected me with fierceness as only a mother and sibling could muster. Growing up in a household where the only attention I ever received was that from women somehow created a bigger divide between my father and me. My father was a man who could work with his hands, and he was a man who could use his hands in a fight as well. My father was a carpenter, and yet I never received the gene with this skill. I simply cannot use my hands to create anything out of wood or any other material.

"Go on, chop that piece of wood, then use the sandpaper to make it smooth," my father one day said.

"Chop it with what?" I asked innocently.

"With these tools, you fool!" he roared.

Needless to state, I silently slipped away as a fool does not know how woodwork tools work, nor is unwise enough to spend time with an angry drunkard. And, I knew that by sticking around he would lose his temper with me and that would lead to disaster, so not unlike a dog kicked once too many, I retreated and retracted in my fantasy world.

Despite the fact that my father and I never saw eye to eye and that there simply was no relationship between the two of us, I always sensed and felt that something was amiss. Although not resentful of my few close friends who had relationships with their fathers, I realised from a very young age that something so special was not present in my life. And I longed for it. My father was not a man of many words so it was useless to try to have a conversation with him around this issue. Not that I would have been able to as I was too young to fully comprehend what was going on.

At school Sis and I, both did exceedingly and exceptionally well. Both of us were valedictorian recipients for our academic prowess! In fact, we excelled at school. Mom never had to remind us to do our homework, and never needed to tell us to study. And, as a result, Mom accepted the fact that we were aware of our responsibilities and she would never need to ask us about this at all. Our report cards, certificates and trophies would be ample proof to her whether we were doing well or not and there was never a need to punish us for our results.

Always keen to share our triumphs at school with Mom, she in return would show our report cards to my father. My father would bestow Sis with praise, even hinting that the apple did not fall far from the tree, but never a word of praise was uttered to me. No praise, no condemnation, just quiet acknowledgement.

"Mom," I said. "Why is it that I never hear a word of praise from Dad at all?"

Caught unawares from a child hardly 10 years old, Mom did not have an answer and chose to circumvent the answer.

"As long as you know you are doing well, that should be the only reward you should ask for in life, my child."

I was not placated by the answer. But it became my motto in life. *Do not expect any praise from anyone, satisfy yourself and measure your satisfaction in the reward.*

And so I would learn to stay out of my father's way. He lived his life, and in only a way a child can, as a child, I lived mine. We hardly spoke, and I never asked him for anything, no money (on the odd occasion when he worked), no permission. Nothing. Anything I needed I would ask Mom. He most of the time, in any case, was inebriated and then became verbally abusive, sometimes physically abusive, but most of the times I managed to stay out of his way. Hide away when he was calling for me, as only in his intoxicated state would he call for me, looking to find some fault with me, or generally just have a good mental or physical melt-down with me. Not going to happen. Stay away was my motto in life, and if asked why you did not react, why, I did not hear you would the answer be all innocently.

Mint punch or brandy. Those were the idols of my father, the treasures he coveted most in life. Without either one, he was nothing, a pitiful being with no dignity or self-respect. But once mint punch or brandy reacquainted themselves with him after time off the binge, my father would become his own hateful self. There were many evenings that we could not sleep, as in his drunken furore, he would call my mother for one chore or the other. Chores that she had to do for the sake of keeping the peace.

"Why, Mom, why do we have to allow him to rule our lives like this?" I one day asked Mom.

"Do not talk about him like this. He is your father," Mom would scold me.

A father? No father to me, I would think to myself, but would not utter these words aloud, as I had far too much love and respect to ever question Mom in those days.

Through all this, I started to see my father as a nuisance. Likewise, I knew he thought of me as inferior, as a freak and as a disappointment. And, he hated me for my inferiority. I was nothing that he was at my age, I did not like anything he liked, we had nothing in common and hence we were as different as strangers could be to one another. I sometimes wondered whether he thought that I was not his child, albeit that the resemblance between Sis and I was remarkably striking. But, I knew one thing for sure: I never wanted to be like him at all. He was no role model to me and I most certainly did not think of him as a hero or as a father. I saw him as someone who tolerated me, and I in return had to avoid and if that was not possible, then only to be tolerant. But never accept.

Then my father started to get sick. Cirrhosis of the liver, the reward paid to him by his idols. This made my father retain water, and he became bloated. The last year of his life, my father realised that he did not have long to live, and he tried to make amends. He tried in an awkward way to reach out to me, and start having odd conversations with me. But for me, it was too late. Ten years of abuse, ten years of nothing but hatred from this man could not be wiped clean in one year, no matter how hard he tried. And I will give this to him, tried he most definitely did. I was not, however,

61

ready or susceptible to his advances. But my father rejecting me all these years left a hole wider than a crater on the moon, and one year was far too little time to fill this crater with love, harmony, acceptance and understanding. Understanding that I was different and that everyone is different. And somewhere in all of this forgiveness was silently asked but quietly rejected.

I came to detest alcohol as I had first-hand experience of how drunkards and inebriates could destroy families. When I look at my father's history, and see that most of his siblings and his family members had a special affection and infinity for the bottle, I promised myself two things. I will never touch alcohol in my life. Never. Not a drop. Not an ounce. And if the Lord should bless me with children one day, I will never be a father to them the way he lacked being a father to me. And to this day, I have never touched alcohol, do not know what a beer tastes like, have no desire to taste what stronger spirits taste like. Sure, I had champagne with orange juice once. It left me cold. I did not acquire the taste, and will never acquire it in my life. Perhaps the consequences of any over-indulgence left the sour taste in my mouth and the incomprehension of how anyone could love or even enjoy a simple drink or two.

A HEADMASTER'S DISMISSAL

I had an absolute blast in primary school. From early on I had shown leadership qualities. Despite the fact, or perhaps because of an alcoholic father who set no example, led no one and was never admired for his accomplishments, after his passing, I had this sense of achieving, wanting to do better and show the world (him perhaps?) that I can do it, despite the adversities I have encountered over the years. In Grade 5 (we used to call it Standard 3 in those days), I was elected to form part of the scholar patrol. This, in essence, required that at seven o'clock in the morning, we would report for duty, take a pole with a stop sign attached to it specifically for scholar patrol purposes, and ensure that traffic passing the school was regulated and scholars were crossing the street in a safe environment. We had one teacher who would test the scholar patrol's nerves, as in those days (the early eighties), the scholar patrol walked into the street and stood directly on the zebra crossing straight in the middle of the road, and stopped traffic to allow the scholars to pass. This teacher, Mr Brown, always stopped very close to your knees and expected you to not flinch. We all took this duty very seriously and executed it with flair. Mr Brown often commented on how proud he was of us and because of our commitment to ensuring the safe passage for our scholars, there was never an incident that took place during that specific year.

In Standard 4 (Grade 6), I was elected to the primary school student council as a prefect. This entailed ensuring that the scholars were all neatly assembled in classroom order every morning for the morning greeting by the headmaster and that during lunch breaks, general order prevailed on the school grounds. We had to make sure that there was no fighting between scholars, no bullying, and the younger scholars who needed assistance or guidance always attended to. Being a prefect was such an accolade and I simply loved it. Yes, at times I also had to take a scholar or two to the headmaster's office for disobedience or misconduct, but for me, the treasure and the reward came from leading a team. We were given specific standards or grades to look after; specific areas on the school grounds to patrol, and this responsibility made me feel wanted and needed.

The following year, I was elected as Head Boy. This was the ultimate honour that could be bestowed on any scholar. Now my duties included leading the boys' group of prefects and ensuring that the roster is attended to in terms of duties and that they fulfilled their duties without fail. Bigger responsibilities. And I ended that year as the Dux Scholar for 1983 in our primary school, meaning I was the best and top performing student in our standard (or grade). I received seven book prizes as well as the Dux Trophy. I was simply delirious. All my hard work had paid off. And I was being recognised. Recognised for my achievements. Recognised for my contribution. Recognised and accepted as an outstanding scholar (as per the engraving on the Dux trophy!).

And then, I went to high school, a different high school than Sis who was one standard ahead of me. Starting Standard 6 (Grade 8) was an absolute disaster. I hated it. Where in primary school, I felt like "Stan the Man", all of a sudden I had to go through an initiation where I had to wear a funny stupid hat, that I had to bow before every senior Matric student I ran into during the course of the day. I hated it. Every day of my life. Going home every afternoon, I would whine and complain to Mom, saying I hate school, I hated it.

Mom would only look at me and say, "Give it time. This is new. You need to adapt. I understand that you don't like change. But you are going to need to adjust, my child, or else you are going to be unhappy all the time."

But I did not want to listen, so I asked Mom to let me change schools and attend the same high school as Sis.

"At least there I would know someone," I reasoned.

But this was not to be. Sis' high school was already filled with its quota of scholars and hence I could not be transferred to the same school. Stuck. As the initiation was over, and I was now a fully-fledged high school scholar, life became a little more bearable; however, I still intensely disliked high school. And this was noticed. Albeit that my grades were great and I continued to perform well and achieve high marks, I did not partake in any sports activities or in any other activities available to scholars to compete and be part of. And this too was noticed.

Some time in my second month at high school, the outgoing headmaster at the time called me to his office for a private conversation. When I was called to his office the first time around, I almost had a heart attack. What did I do wrong? Why am I in trouble? What does he want from me?

"Come in, young man," the headmaster called me from the entrance to his office. "Please take a seat."

For a long time, he looked at me, with kindness (I hoped) in his eyes. "You are a troubled and conflicted child, my son," he started off saying.

"Sir?" I croaked.

"Something is eating at you, lad. And this is not good for you or your reputation which you start to build the moment you join our school or for making friends and building relationships."

"Sir?" I squirmed. I did not understand where the conversation was leading.

"Yes, boy. We as a school body have noticed. And we are concerned. So what is eating you?" he asked, not unkindly.

"N-nothing sir," I stammered.

"Young man, please allow me to give you some advice. Son, I am an old man, and my time at this wonderful establishment is ending. I know every scholar in my school. I know everything that I need to know about every one of them. Where they come from, what their parents do, how well they performed at primary school, how well they are performing now. What extramural activities they take part in. Their achievements. Everything. Do you follow, son?"

"I… I think so, s-sir." I managed to whisper.

"So, my boy. What I am trying to say is that in my school, we make no distinction from one child to another. Everyone that joined our community here is part of it. We care about their well-being and their performance, but we also care about their social skills.

"I know where you come from, son. I know what you come from as well. But I also know you have potential. Use it, Son. Don't waste your God-given talent and brains. I understand that you are overwhelmed right now, but son, accept this, embrace this. Become part of it. Don't isolate yourself. Make new friends. But, son, enjoy it. You only ever get to do this once."

I had absolutely nothing to say. I was gob-smacked. Where in primary school, all my friends were relatively in the same position I was in, living in Tranquillity, being poor, or not so poor, but never rich. So we all had the same background. Going to high school, was quite different. Here I met children who came from affluent suburbs I had never heard of, parents who dropped their children off at school in cars that showed wealth and prosperity. Children who could take part in every activity the school offered, as their parents had the money to allow it. To buy them the gear and the clothing required for the special activities. I could never compete. I could never be their equal. So I was determined to do well in school, better than most of them, but never befriend them. For then I would have to let them know where I am from. And that I simply could not do. But… Here was a man, a headmaster, who made it sound that I should look beyond these obstacles and partake in what I believed I was good at. And make friends. New friends.

This was a slow awakening. For my first year at high school, I remained a loner, other than at the odd occasion mingling with one or two of my primary school friends. But we outgrew each other. School, however, became more tolerable and I continued to excel in my grades. And the talk that I had with the now retired headmaster always resounded and replayed in my head during that first year at high school.

The following year I was placed with a new group of scholars, and for the first time felt part of this group. Granted, they still came from affluent areas, but somehow, we never spoke about our backgrounds. This was never important. What probably made me grow close to these fellow scholars was the fact that we wanted to be the best performing class of Standard 7 (Grade 9). And I was part of this challenge. And no, we did not only compete academically with the other Standard 7s, we also competed in sport and cultural activities. And I had to partake, so in the beginning, I started to do the cultural activities more, like recitation, choir, and being part of the debate team. This needed no special gear or any funds, so I easily managed to take part in these challenges. And did exceptionally well.

And so for the next three years, up to Standard 9 (Grade 11), most of these scholars remained part of my class, so to me they became class friends. And I even made two very good friends that knew where I lived, but I always went to their houses, never they to mine.

By this time, we had a new headmaster appointed. This new headmaster was nothing like the previous retired headmaster. More interested in school funds and funding projects than the genuine well-being of scholars, after all, in his opinion, that was the job of the teachers; he was not loved much, but feared a great lot by most scholars. In those days, corporal punishment was allowed, and he never hesitated to take his cane and to give you three of the best.

So at the end of my penultimate year at high school, the school decided to send all the potential leaders who would be elected to the Student Council the following year to a development and evaluation camp. This meant a weekend away where these potential leaders would be challenged and their leadership abilities assessed, and then the top twenty (ten boys and ten girls) then selected as the prefects in our final year of high school.

Forty scholars were elected, and I was included as one of the potential prefects to be evaluated. Again, I had that warm sense of accomplishment the day my name was read to attend the leadership camp as again I was being recognised for my abilities and for who I am. The camp, however, was not free, and students had to pay a hefty amount for the weekend away. Mom did everything possible to allow me to pay for the weekend away, but the day before the closing date of all consent and waiver forms being handed in together with the payment, we, unfortunately, could not manage to accumulate half of the funds required to pay. The only thing that was left to do was for me to withdraw.

Mom did not want to hear about this.

"This is an opportunity for you to again serve on the school council. You have worked so hard for this," Mom cried.

"Mom, the fact that I was recognised is award enough," I said, knowing full well that this was not the truth.

But I could not blame Mom, and neither could I hurt Mom. Mom tried her best, but we simply could not make ends meet. I also refused for Mom to borrow money from anyone, as it would put her in an embarrassing situation on the one hand, but also put pressure on her to find the funds to repay the debt from her Fafi commission. This was something I simply could not ask of Mom.

Sis also had only started working and had new expenses that she had to cover, ranging from bus fare to clothing accounts, as she now needed to be dressed for the working environment. So money simply wasn't available.

So the following day, our class teacher collected all the funds and the returned consent notes.

"I did not receive yours," the teacher reminded me in front of the class.

"I decided to not attend, Ma'am," I answered the teacher. Shocked murmurs went up in the class and even a few words of dissent from my fellow friends and scholars.

"Please stay behind after class," the teacher informed me rather curtly.

"But, ma'am," I started.

"Don't 'But ma'am' me, young man." Stalemate. I had no choice. I now had to tell the teacher why it was that I could not go.

"Do you realise that you have a very good opportunity of being elected to the Student Council. That although 50% of the votes are made up of fellow scholars, the remaining 50% will be votes from the teachers. By not going, you are doing yourself a grave injustice," the teacher told me.

"Ma'am, my intention is not to upset anyone. However, I simply cannot go."

"Young man, over the years I have been watching your progress with a keen eye." She went on to my astonishment.

"I always knew you had what it takes to be a leader, to lead a team and to set an example. By not going, you are losing the chance and wasting the opportunity to show the rest of them what I see in you."

"Thank you, ma'am, I really appreciate it. But I simply cannot go."

"I am no fool. From the day they announced the camp and what it would cost, I knew that you were in a pickle. If you want to, let me speak to the headmaster. We will find a way around this."

"No, ma'am!" I cried out. "There is no need to speak to the headmaster. I cannot go, and that is it."

"Listen to me. I wanted your consent to speak to the headmaster, but I will be damned if I am going to allow you to steamroll this opportunity. Now I am telling you I will have a discussion with the headmaster, as you will attend the camp if I have anything to do about this."

"Ma'am, please don't. This is humiliating enough as it is. I cannot risk anyone knowing that the headmaster had to make a special concession for me to go because we could not afford the fees."

"Oh, dear me! Pride is a wonderful thing. But pride should never get in your way. And you should be proud of your background, where you come from, what you have achieved. And what you will achieve in future. Never be too proud to admit defeat. Never be too proud to say, I cannot. Be and remain true to yourself. And of course, no-one will know, as this will be a matter between the headmaster and me," my class teacher continued.

"Ma'am, unless you have lived my life, you will not understand what it is to be poor, to go hungry, to be looked down on, to feel inferior."

I then started to cry, feeling sorry for myself, for Mom, Sis and the circumstances we were living in.

My class teacher did not say another word. She took me in her arms, and quietly consoled me. Before the end of the day, I was called to her office, and she advised me that it was all sorted out. If I had the necessary consent forms signed, there is no payment required from me. Mom could sign that afternoon, and I could return the consent form the following day. I hugged my class teacher, conflicted. On the one hand, I was absolutely delighted that I had the opportunity to attend and potentially be chosen to serve on the Student Council. On the other hand, I felt gutted, as again, poverty followed me like a shadow, and when you least expect it, you are overshadowed by it, confronted by it and cannot hide from it. But the delight had the upper hand this time around, albeit bittersweet.

Two weeks later, the Friday afternoon after school, we all got on a bus; off to the development and evaluation camp we went. The camp was about three hours away from school, so when we arrived, we were assigned rooms for the weekend. We then were told to get dressed for supper and had to be in the dining room hall within an hour.

After supper, we were divided into groups, and we were given Shakespearian quotations that we had to memorise and then act out accordingly. Each group competed within the groups, first to find the best orator, and then the winners in each group then would compete against each other to finally award the best orator of the evening.

Our group received the quote "For Brutus is an honourable man" from Julius Caesar. The instructions were that we had to repeat the phrase three times, once, making a statement, once making an announcement and once casting doubt on Brutus' honour. After competing within my team, I was selected by my team as the top orator that had to compete against the nine other groups' chosen speakers. At the end of the evening, I won with flying colours. I could convince a group, I could simply make a statement or I could cast doubt on a group. I was commended by my team and by the other teams as well as by the teachers and judges. What a night. On a very high, I went to bed quite late that evening, ready for the next day's activities.

The following morning we had breakfast, then we attended a lecture for a few hours on leadership skills where we were observed in terms of how we interact with groups, our answers to questions raised and in general, how we would react in certain circumstances. Thereafter we had lunch, and then had some free time to explore the camp or swim in the swimming pool. Early that evening, we congregated in our groups again, and the task assigned to our groups that evening was that we had to hold a debate where one party had to debate against the other. Instead of giving one the opportunity to talk and then the other raises their points, it was decided that both speakers would raise their issues at the same time. The one who came out the strongest, the most convincing and who could debate for two minutes flat without stopping to think about what to say next would be the winner. Again, my team chose me as the overall winner, and again, later that evening, with resounding success, I was crowned as the top debater and speaker of the evening. I lost my voice with all the debating, but it was worth losing, as the boy from Tranquillity was crowned as an overall natural leader, speaker, orator and yes, even winner and conqueror! Never before could I remember a time that I felt this elated. And all my fellow scholars, all wished me well, not one of them begrudged me my success of the weekend.

Sunday morning we had breakfast, and then set out on our way back to school in the bus transporting the forty scholars and ten teachers and headmaster. A while into the drive, the headmaster called me to come and sit next to him. I gladly went, nothing could spoil this weekend for me, and as the headmaster surely noticed my prowess and knew that I had the support of my fellow scholars and teachers, surely this would only be a good conversation to have.

"So," he started off saying, "did you enjoy the development camp?"

"Oh, yes, sir. It was an absolutely amazing weekend," I whispered, as my voice was still not healed after all the excitement and shouting during the debate contest.

"You know that this is but one step in the leadership evaluation process?" he enquired from me.

"Yes, sir," I croaked. "I know that the rest of the Standard 9 and Matric students still get to vote, as does the teacher body."

"Do you think that you stand a good chance?"

"I really couldn't tell, sir. It all depends on who the teachers and scholars see as the right leaders to lead our school team next year."

"Why do you think they should choose you, over and above some other deserving candidates?" he asked. I looked around, but no one was particularly interested in our conversation.

"I don't know, sir. Perhaps because I am a good orator, because I can debate a point well and that I feel that I can give guidance, Sir?"

"Okay. Hypothetically speaking. We have a scholar who is at the farthest side of the school fence and you happen to catch him smoking during lunch break. What do you do?"

"If it is his first offence, sir, I would warn him to cut it out and advise him that he knows the rules."

"What if he continues smoking and he ignores your warning?"

"I would walk up to him, sir and give him one last warning."

"And if he still refuses to quit smoking?"

"Then, sir, I will have no alternative but to report him for two transgressions, one for ignoring an instruction and the other for breaking one of the school ground rules."

"And if this scholar is from a wealthy family?" he asked me?

"What about it, sir? I don't understand what his background has to do with his transgression?" I was starting to get uncomfortable. Where was this leading to?

"Well, let's see, with your background and all, here we have a scholar from an affluent area, and he is being told by a boy from a very poor family and trashy suburb to follow the rules. Why in the world would he want to listen to someone who is not his equal?"

"Sir?"

"Oh, come on! Surely, you are not that naive that you think people don't know that the school sponsored your camping trip. That people don't know where you live and where you are from?"

"Well, sir. If they know, and this is the reason they ignore me, I will still report them as I said before."

Gutted, hurt and confused by the remarks made by the headmaster, but I had nowhere to go. Stuck. How would the people know that the school sponsored me? Who would have told them? Why? But I will not ask him, I will not let him know that he touched a nerve. I will not show that his words hurt me, that he humiliated me by even having this conversation with me.

"And if he taunts you. About not having money and that he will not listen to a poor boy from a poor family from a poor suburb, what will you do then?"

"Sir?"

"What will you do? Surely you will get angry?"

"Yes, sir. I will be angry. But I will not let that get in the way of me doing my duties."

"So you will ignore his remarks?"

"Sir, I most definitely will try. Sir, I believe in the old saying of 'sticks and stones…'"

"Mmm. You're a clever one, aren't you?" he asked.

I kept quiet and felt it best to treat the question as rhetorical.

"So we have this rich boy, good looking dude, popular guy, and his only fault is he likes smoking. He gets caught by you, and he taunts you. You are about to turn your back on him to go and report him, when he grabs your jacket and punches you one against the cheek. What do you do?"

"Sir, I will need to defend myself first. For if I try to walk away, he may continue punching me," I said.

"Okay, so you will hit him back. That is what you are saying?"

"Sir, I will only hit him back if that is the last and only alternative."

"Okay, I see. Thank you, you can return to your seat now."

I guess that something in my face must have shown the rest of the group that the discussion did not go well, as they all asked about it. I shrugged and in my croaky voice simply said that he wanted to know how I would react in certain circumstances, but did not elaborate too much on our discussion.

When we arrived back at the school, I grabbed my bags and started walking home, as there was no public transport on a Sunday that would run past the school and be on the bus route that would take me home. Walking the more than three and a half kilometres home, I kept on replaying the conversation with the headmaster in my head. I had a growing sense of discomfort that somehow something that I did at the camp ensured or caused that he disliked me. But for the life of me, I could not place my finger on it. Surely, he did not expect his son to win, who was also in Standard 9 and elected to attend? Surely not? It was a given that his son would be elected in any event, so it could not be that? Was it the fact that a teacher spoke up on my behalf and managed to get me to go to the camp? Did he not want me to attend? I simply did not have the answers. And for the rest of that Sunday, the discomfort gnawed at me like a growing ulcer, festering. But an answer I knew I would not get on this one.

Two weeks later, my class teacher asked me to stay behind after class.

"My dear," she said. "What I am about to tell you is in absolute confidence. I need you to promise me that you will not utter a word to anyone. For if you do, I stand the risk of losing my job."

"Ma'am?" I managed to utter, quite confused. Why would a teacher confide in me and then do it at the risk of losing her job?

"Oh, my. I, I, I need to apologise to you first. Had I not insisted you attend that dreadful leadership camp, I would not have been in the position I am today.

"The headmaster has called a special meeting for the teacher body that will elect the Student Council for next year. He made it very clear to the teacher body, to us, that you are not to be elected by any of us for the Student Council."

I went cold and felt a hollow feeling in the pit of my stomach. What was going on?

"Ma'am, did he say why?" I asked, feeling numb and shell-shocked.

"He mentioned that he tested you on the way from the camp and the answers he received from you were less than satisfactory. That he could not allow the reputation of the school to be tarnished by electing a scholar with a lesser background than the others. That the Parent-Teacher Association will simply not condone it. And that you are prone to violence."

Dumbfounded, I could only stare at my class teacher. Rejected again. For being poor. To protect some more affluent scholar's pride and ego. Violent? Me? By only answering that if the last resort was to defend myself, I am now being branded as violent.

Clearly, the headmaster had an intense disliking in me, and that I represented everything he loathed. But for him to exert pressure on the teacher body to ensure that I am not elected was downright mean. He did not want to risk the chance that I would get chosen, so he coerced the teacher body to go along with his verdict. I hated him at that moment as much as I ever hated my father. I hated the position I was in and I hated the fact that there was nothing I could do about it. Nothing at all.

"Ma'am," I started, "I will never know the reason why you were prompted to tell me today. I can only..." and then I burst out crying. This time around, I did not want to be consoled, so I fled. Hiding in the boys' bathrooms until such time that I could compose myself, raw tears flowed down my cheeks, rivers of pain and sorrow. All that I had aspired to flushed down the drain in one single decision made by one single person. With no regard to whether I could be a good leader or not. My background counted against me, plain and simple. I was my own enemy it seems, as my victory over my fellow scholars showed that a boy from nothing could rise from the ashes of poverty and beat others who were prepped for this their entire lives. And that the community simply was not ready, and never will be ready to have the poor conquer the wealthy.

A while later after I settled down somewhat, seeing as I was late for my next class I decided to give it a skip altogether. My classmates would explain that I was kept behind, so there would be no recourse. Although my classmates wanted to know what happened, I could not let anyone know and mentioned something about me attending a career seminar to decide which field of study I wanted to pursue. This was not entirely a lie, as my class teacher has been doing this with all the scholars who indicated that they would further their studies after finishing high school. This was a good enough reason to stop my classmates from prying.

I went back after school to talk to my class teacher again. I assured her that I was grateful for her telling me now, as there would not have been a worst rejection had I sat waiting to be called out as one of the Student Council Prefects and my name was not called out. The voting period would commence the following week, so I had enough time to prepare for this eventuality.

In order to save face in front of my classmates and other keen supporters, I announced to them that I had considered being a prefect and that I enjoyed being amongst the scholars too much during breaks to still attend to others. I announced that I requested to withdraw, but as it was too late, I appealed to them to please not vote for me. Whether they did vote for me or not, I will never know, but a month after the camp, and two weeks after having that confidential but soul-drenching discussion with my class teacher, the Student Council was announced during assembly. And although I hoped against all hope that somehow, somewhere, someone would have been able to change the headmaster's mind, my name was never called. Effectively, I was left out in the cold.

I thoroughly enjoyed my final year in high school, albeit always with a sense of melancholy and humiliation. My classmates and supporters all were disappointed in my not serving on the Council, but they never questioned or discussed this fact with me ever again. I was able to spend time with my few close school friends who were not on the Student Council, and other friends who were on the Council from time to time looked me up on the school grounds. I tried to hold my head up high, never once talking about the fact that the headmaster rejected me for his own very personal reasons. It was a bitter pill to swallow but made me more determined to prove him wrong.

As every Matric student is involved in the initiation of the new Standard 6 scholars, I was no exception. But I promised myself one thing, my initiates would have an entry and a taste of high school quite differently to what I had. I had a total of six scholars who were to carry my bag, books and blazer and had to be around me at all times when classes were out, during breaks and during rehearsals. I never abused my power; I made the initiation as tranquil as possible. And on the day that they were welcomed as true high school attendees and no longer as initiates, I called them all together and spoke to them from the heart:

"Today marks the beginning of your true entrance and acceptance into high school. And it is also a transformation for each and every one of you. A transformation from primary to secondary school, from being children to becoming teenagers, from being in charge to starting all over. During the next five years, you will encounter several of the trials and tribulations that high school has to offer. But remember one thing. Always be true to yourselves, no matter what. And that all men and women are created equal before God. Forget about race, background, education or wealth; remember, at the end of the day, we are all human and all the same. Enjoy your high school years. Excel in whatever it is that you do. Be humble, be gracious, be thankful. And in five years' time, when you stand where I am standing today, and you had some new scholars that you had to initiate and be responsible for. Always let them retain their dignity. Always compare your experience with that of your peers. And provide them with a similar transition."

During my final year, I avoided the headmaster like the plague, and he somehow embraced the fact that our interaction was limited. After writing the final exams, arriving at school to get our results and final report cards, it was announced that I was overall the second best achieving scholar of our school for that year. I shared this place with six other scholars. And while the headmaster was boasting and taking the credit for our achievements, congratulating each student and their parents, I quietly walked away without speaking to him or ever accepting any word of praise from him. One of my fellow scholars caught up to me

"Where were you?" he asked. "The headmaster was looking for you and wanted to see you."

"He can go to hell for all I care," was my retort, pretending not to notice the surprised look on his face. What could the headmaster do? I was no longer a high school scholar, and I no longer needed to listen to him or to obey him. He now means even less to me, as I am finally free of him.

Fifteen years later, I was invited to a school reunion. It was great fun to see how my fellow scholars have changed, and how many of them had made successes of their lives, had children and lived life in the conventional way. And how many of the teachers still attended the reunion. The headmaster was also there, and although I did try to avoid him but it was inevitable that I would run into him and have a discussion with him.

"So, here you are," he said to me. "Fifteen years later. I have followed your career with great interest. I notice that you have advanced quite substantially in your career and you have a very important leadership role now in your organisation. You must clearly be doing quite well for yourself then, driving a luxury car and heading a division in your organisation."

I was surprised at just how much he knew about me, and couldn't help but think that if he had a conscience, surely this must have been hounding him all these years. Maybe he regretted his actions, actions he never knew that I was aware of. And would never know.

"Yes," I said. "Contrary to what you had thought would happen to a poor boy, with a poor family from a poor suburb."

With that, I turned around, walked away and left him standing there, stewing in his own thoughts. This was one man who ruined a grand opportunity for me, but perhaps as a result of him, my father and other influences in my life, this all drove me to make a success of my life, which without the Lord's guidance, I know would not have been possible. I persevered. Sir, you see, tenacity pays off, regardless of where you come from.

I never did see him again. As for my class teacher who told me about what happened, unsurprisingly she also followed my career and progress in life. And that evening of our fifteenth school re-union, the moment she laid eyes on me, she started to cry. I took her arm and hooked it in mine, and she and I walked the school grounds in silence. Comfortable silence. There was no need to talk, as words were unnecessary. One person, who showed she believed in me, never stopped believing in me and who trusted in me and my abilities unconditionally. To make the pain of rejection lesser. And in hindsight, succeeded in it. And with her actions, and with us walking there for almost twenty minutes that evening, conversation being unnecessary and superfluous, the knowledge of acceptance by so many slowly started to fill the gap of rejection by so few.

A FRIENDSHIP NO MORE

I always was a bit of a loner, for many reasons. Mostly due to the fact that being poor, staying in a poor neighbourhood and not having a father that I could look up to and do father and son things with, being brought up by Mom and Sis and being with them most of the times made me somewhat of an anomaly. So I found it quite difficult to truly make friends, and when I do make friends, and I see that they accepted me for who and what I was, then I would give it my all, especially when I was older.

When I was at university for the first time, I really became true friends with someone that was also living in Tranquillity at the time. I would still frequent José and Catia's cafe, and from time to time they would have these Atari games that you play which would cost you twenty cents a game. This was such an escape from reality that I became quite good at a few games that we played. And at times, the Atari games would allow dual players at the same time. And this is how Matt and I became friends.

Our friendship ran deep, and the trust between us was rock solid. We started dating girls, swam at the public swimming pool together, went out together, watched movies and had a lot of fun. For me, for the first time in my life, I had someone who understood me for whom I was, and accepted me for whom I am. He became my best friend. Matt, well built for his age, black hair and green eyes, was only a year younger than I, but this was no problem in our friendship bond. Tranquillity became our playground, and we frequented this playground often and with vigour.

So the years passed, and we continued to be best friends. When Matt had to write his Matric exams, I was the one he called upon to assist him with some of the subjects that he struggled with. I loved doing this for my mate Matt. He passed Matric with flying colours, the same year that I finished my first year at university.

As with any friendship, there will be disagreements, but none that we could not sort out. Over the years, I have learned that the best way to address a problem is not to ignore it. Talk about it, and get it resolved and move on. No problem is insurmountable, and none can be of such a nature that one cannot find a workable solution for this. This strengthened the friendship that Matt and I had.

During his final school year, Matt met a girl that he fell hard for. He really loved this girl and he gave it everything to make the relationship work between them. This was no puppy love, this was true love in the truest sense that one can experience between two people. And I was extremely happy for Matt. Jen was an absolute knockout stunner. Long blonde hair, a body to die for, legs that simply never ended and the most beautiful piercing blue eyes ever, she was the envy of many a girl. And she cared about Matt almost as much as he cared about her. But she, unfortunately, had a range of suitable suitors who would vie for her hand in love. This did not stop or deter Matt at all. Love doesn't ask why, doesn't ask who and doesn't at first judge or reject. Naturally, Jen and I became good friends, as she chose my mate Matt, despite the other guys trying to court her. And the three of us would often spend some time together. Jen understood how deep the friendship was between Matt and me, and she embraced and accepted it as part of the young man she fell in love with. I also had a steady girlfriend at that time, but Jen and Tania did not really get along, so all four of us getting together was quite infrequent. Still, Matt and I kept our friendship going, and I was his confidante, as he was mine.

Once Matt finished high school, he was called to complete his compulsory military service conscription. Matt asked me to look after Jen while he was away. This I solemnly promised him to do. Whenever Matt had some weekend or longer breaks that allowed him to return home temporarily, he would spend almost all of his time with Jen. But before going home after a visit with Jen, irrespective of the time in the morning, he would simply stop outside our house, knock on my bedroom window, and I would wake up, and the two of us would either go for a drive or spend a few minutes together, catching up or discussing issues at hand. This was how great our friendship was, and we both worked hard at it. Matt would tell me about his military service, would confide in me if something was wrong between him and Jen, would ask me if I heard rumours, and if we went for a drive, we would drive until sunrise, after which he would drop me off, and I would get ready for university.

At times, the car would break down. Without a word, I would get out of the car and start to push and we always got the car going again. Sometimes I slipped in rainy weather, as the car had a habit of breaking down especially during torrential showers, but I never did mind. This was time with my mate, my pal, my best friend, and my brother. And I treasured it.

And Matt was not afraid to use his hands. He was slow to get angry, but once he got angry, he would not hesitate to use his fists to protect himself or protect the things he cared about. Matt was an amiable guy, and everyone liked him, and many regarded him as a friend.

Sadly, being apart from Matt for too long a period of time took its toll on Jen. She simply could not wait on Matt for the period of his conscription. Tania and I ended our relationship a year after Matt started doing his military service and we remained good friends, so I was in between girlfriends when he finished his military service. It was a tough time for Matt, as Jen found someone else, but first love never dies, and on several occasions, they tried to rekindle their love. But Matt simply could not get over the fact that Jen had some other love interests whilst he was protecting our borders and completing compulsory national military service. It was not as if he had a choice, nor that he deliberately could not spend time with her. But despite the fact that they tried on several occasions to move past this volatile point, in the end, the best for both of them was to stay apart, as together they tore each other apart. However, I never was convinced throughout our friendship that Matt ever got over Jen, and likewise, I believed that Jen regretted her straying, but could not find the right bridge to close the gap with.

Through all this heartache and pain, Matt confided in me, and I was there for him. Matt was like a brother to me, a brother I never had, and as Matt accepted me with all my faults and differences, I would have laid my life down for Matt if ever it came to that. Inseparable we were. And friends we would remain I believed until the end of days.

I started working right after Matt completed his military service, and Matt was scouring for suitable jobs. After six months of searching and applying for roles, Matt was called for an interview as a manager at one of the nightclubs we frequented often. Matt was given a form to complete on why he would be the right person for his job, and some crazy psychological questions asked, probably to determine Matt's state of mind and if he was psychotic and whether he would not be the cause for a lawsuit if appointed. Matt and I laughed about the silly questions, but we were realistic enough to know that it was serious enough and that the nightclub had a reputation that they wanted to uphold. So we answered the questionnaire truthfully and went through some of the answers in case Matt would be asked similar questions in the interview. Matt simply aced it and was appointed immediately.

The hours that Matt had to work at the nightclub did not interfere with our friendship time, and during this time Matt met several young women that he made an impression on, and they made a similar impression on him. I was also playing the field, not really looking for something seriously, as between work and tutoring lessons, I had very little time for a full-time girlfriend.

And soon, Matt started to fall for someone he met at the club. He swooned about her, raved about how she made him feel, and for the first time since Jen, it seemed as if Matt was going to be happy again. And Hilary did make him happy. The first time I met Hilary I simply knew that Matt was her first love, the way she looked at him and the fact that she simply adored him. And as with Jen, Hilary and I also became very good friends, and whenever we could, Matt, Hillary and I would spend time together. Although Hilary was not in the same beauty category as Jen, she nevertheless was a looker and fell very easy on the eye. Light brown hair, green eyes and a prominent nose, Hilary did not necessarily stand out in a crowd at all. But the moment she started to speak, her bubbly personality and infectious laugh simply attracted everyone and she was absolutely adorable.

"She is the right one for me, mate," Matt gushed!

"Take it slow, bro! Just now you pop the big question and have a string of kids around you!"

"Since Jen, I did not think that I would ever feel this way about a girl again. But I do. I am. And it's crazy," he opined.

Hilary with the green eyes, the drop-dead figure, the long brown hair. Hilary who only had eyes for Matt. And there was chemistry. A lot of chemistry between them, electrical charges would go off when you saw them together. And when they danced, it was as if they became one. Lithe, light-footed, dancing to the rhythm of the music. Simply beautiful to watch. And to know that these two special people were part of my life made me extremely happy. And within a flash, Matt and Hilary celebrated their first anniversary together as lovers, friends and partners. And they started talking about moving in together soon, as both had stable jobs, and although Matt's job required him to be out at night, his shifts mostly started around eleven at night, so ample time for them to spend together before Hilary had to go to bed for work.

As Matt and I were friends for many years by this time, we were also regulars at each other's homes. I enjoyed spending time with his family, his mother, father, three sisters and two broth-ers, as they were quite a big family. And Matt got along fine with Mom and Sis. I would spend more time at Matt's, as it was just the way our friendship developed, and I even spent times there when he was finishing his military service or when he worked an extra shift at the nightclub.

One evening after work, and after tutor lessons that left me quite exhausted, I had dinner at home and then went over to Matt's house. Matt was getting ready for work later that evening, so it was going to be a brief visit and he and I would take a ride later on, he then would drop me off at home before he would pop in at Hilary's and then would go to work. Walking in, Matt's sister Phoebe was busy doing her homework, and the other four sib-lings were somewhere busy in the house. But I immediately had an uneasy feeling and I sensed some tension but did not know where it was coming from. The conversation was strained, and Matt did not seem like his own self. Only Phoebe was her usual self.

"Did you hear that Hilary and Matt had a fight?" Phoebe asked me in her own innocent way as I walked in. From the corner of my eye, I caught their mother in the hallway, shaking her head as if to say to Phoebe to not let me know about the incident.

"No, Phoebes," I said. "Something serious?"

I tried to convince myself that the headshake was not aimed at me, that I was imagining things that were not taking place. These were my friends, I was practically a family member. Surely there were no secrets between us where it concerned my best mate?

"Nah, nothing much that they cannot sort out between them," Phoebe answered me. "I just thought you also heard and knew."

"Phoebes," I said. "I am sure that if it is important enough, Matt will tell me about it. Rather tell me about your day."

Phoebe went into a long-winded explanation of how her day went, and although I nodded and "ummed" and "ahhed" in the right places and hopefully at the right times, my mind was racing. For the first time in our six-year friendship, something was amiss. Matt did not confide in me. Why I did not know, and therefore could not wait for us to take our ride so that I could talk to him about it. Phoebe did a one eighty on me, and their mother did not want me to know what was going on.

Matt sensed that I wanted to get out of the house and have a chat in private with him to find out what has taken place at work. He, therefore, tried as far to be unobtrusive, but he wanted to delay our evening ride so that there was not enough time before he went to Hilary and then off to work. But I was restless, and by nature impatient, so eventually said, "Matt, shall we go for a ride and get a Coke at the café as it is getting late?"

He couldn't really reject this request without letting on what was bugging him, so we eventually left for that Coke at José and Catia's.

As we got in the car, I immediately pounced upon him, wanting to know what was troubling my best friend.

"Hey, mate! What's up?"

"It's nothing," Matt said to me.

"Don't you tell me this is nothing. You treat me like shit, your mother is annoyed that Phoebes has mentioned it and you are brooding. So, no, I am sorry but this is not nothing. And since when do we not share and talk about what is bothering us?" I asked of Matt.

"Drop it, mate," Matt said to me. "I don't want to talk about it."

This was completely unknown territory for me. Caught unawares by his outburst and reaction, I silently brooded while we drank our Cokes, tried to make some small talk, but mostly sat there quietly with not much to say.

"Time for me to go," Matt said. "Let me go and drop you off first."

"Thanks," I said, "but I think I will rather walk home. Lots on my mind."

"Suit yourself." And without a word further, Matt got in his car and drove off.

Dejected, I walked home, racking my brain to try and find an answer for Matt's behaviour. Surely, best friends don't treat each other this way, I tried to rationalise. Sure, we don't share everything, but as we were best friends, brothers in fact just not by blood, when something bad happened to one, we usually would talk about it. And when he and Hilary had their differences in the past, he would tell me even ask me for guidance or advice. But this was something that clearly the family did not want me to know about. Why? And how do I go about finding out what was wrong? I did not want Phoebe to get into trouble or put her on the spot, as I knew she would tell me if I probed long enough. I also did not have the right to impose on Hilary and contact her to find out what was going on, for even though we were close friends, there are boundaries that one simply cannot overstep. No, I decided, I would wait this one out and see where this leads.

The next evening I went to Matt's folks' place again, but he had already left for work. He was working a double shift I was informed by his mother. I left shortly after talking to his mother, not sure on what the best way was to get this resolved. Whatever *this* was. But for him to work a double shift meant he was not spending time with Hilary, and that was bad indeed. This was not just a lover's tiff, but what could be so bad that I was left out in the cold?

Around three o'clock the next morning, I heard that old familiar sound of Matt getting out of his car and knocking on my bedroom window. I got up, walked out of the house and got into Matt's car.

"I got some crap with Hillary that I don't know how to make right," Matt said to me.

"I figured," I said to him, peeved off because of what happened and also still groggy from being woken so early on a weekday, which meant a workday.

"Everybody thinks that you are at fault for the crap in the first place," Matt said to me.

"Whaaat? But that is ludicrous!" One actually could hear my jaw drop to the ground. All grogginess left me in a flash. "Who is everybody?" I asked incredulously.

"Listen, mate. I don't want you to confront anybody on this. I don't even want anyone to know that I spoke to you about this. Also, stay away from Hilary, right now I don't need any further complications in my life. You know how you are and how you get when you are mad. Right now I need to handle this my way."

All that I could do was nod my head, silently acquiescing. This is bad. I went cold inside.

Matt opened up and started saying, "You know that I from time to time find certain girls impressionable at the club. Some of them openly flirt with me. Others invite me back to their places."

I did not say a word. I listened to a tale that I knew well. Where was this leading to?

"At times, whilst on shift, I did go to some of their places, make out and then go back to the nightclub again. It was nothing. It meant nothing. Innocent fun. That's all.

"Well, somebody saw me leave the club the one night and saw my car at the one chick's house. They somehow either know Hilary or knew that she is my girl, so they phoned her and told her that I was not at work all the time as she is made to believe. And that my car was parked at the one broad's house."

"And I am being accused of the one running and telling tales about you to Hilary? I didn't even know that you were messing around," I asked incredulously and just looked at him with open disbelief. "For what possible reason? Surely Hilary told you it was not me who phoned her."

"It was bad, mate. And it got heated between us." Matt continued, "Hilary was all hysterical. She did not want me to touch her or allow me to try and explain that it was nothing. That I loved her and only her. A simple transgression, that was all. And when I asked her who told her she told me it doesn't matter who. All that matters is that it is the truth. That she has never been this hurt in her life and that she is a fool, as everyone knew but no one bothered to let her in on the secret. She then chased me away and said she never wanted to see me again."

Matt silently broke down, the last words caught in his throat and uttered with despair. I allowed him time to settle down, thinking that I did not know it was this bad. I knew he flirted, but I did not know that it was this serious. And now he got caught. Why did he do it? Did he not learn from the hurt he experienced first-hand with Jen?

"You know that girls dig me more than they do you, mate. People say this is the reason why you got someone to phone

Hilary. You cannot stand it that I am earning a decent living, having a great girlfriend that I planned on moving in with and in the meantime also having some great fun too."

Ooomph. Another blow, straight from the left field, blindsided and unexpected. What a blow. It felt as if I was hit right in the stomach and I almost doubled over.

"Who are these people that you are referring to?" I asked.

"It doesn't matter at all. It makes no difference. But what they say does make sense."

"So let me get this straight. You are telling me that several people all agree that it could only be me who has done this?" I asked totally incredulous.

"Well, yeah, when I tell them what I think, they seem to agree with me."

"Ok, so when you tell them what you think, does this mean that you have been the one thinking it all along and looking for confirmation from other people around you?"

"Well, yeah!" Matt confirmed.

"These people confirming your suspicions are fools and you are a bigger fool to believe the crap that you just uttered. You don't know what you are talking about," I retaliated.

"Your life is no contest to me. I only ever want you to be happy and to succeed. Amazingly, I need to ask, do you actually believe it? That you have been thinking it and chewing on it. But knowing me and after all these years of friendship, really, do you really believe that I would be capable of such a heinous act?" I continued to ask him.

"At this stage, I simply don't know what to believe."

"Well, I think with the things you just said, and the way you have reacted the last few days clearly speak volumes. Somehow I must have done something, or someone must have said something to you in the past that you now do believe that I had a part in it."

"I don't know, mate. Who else would do such a thing?"

"Grow up, Matt. Now that you are caught you feel all sorry for yourself, and automatically need to find a scapegoat and who better than me? Your best mate. Being jealous of you? What a joke! Trying to break up the relationship between you and Hilary. Why would I want to do that, Matt?"

"I… I am confused, mate. But Hilary told me that she saved the message to remind her of what a jerk I am. I asked her to listen to the saved recording. She said I should bugger off, she is not going to let me know who ratted me out. I said to her I had a right to confront the liar who is trying to get between us. She said that it would take a lot of convincing from my side, as through all this I did not deny nor confirmed the allegations made. And that is all the proof she needed."

Relief swept through me. This would be a way for them to see that I had no hand in this, that I was not guilty of any of this and that I was wrongly accused, judged, found guilty and sentenced.

"So where to from here, Matt?" I asked.

"Don't overreact, mate."

Overreact? Me? When they kept it away from me and when they believed that I had a reason to do this. That I was jealous of Matt's escapades with ladies. And that he had it all and I did not? But I kept quiet and told myself to contain my anger. This is my best friend, for six years we have been brothers, only separated by blood but not by bond. The best way forward for all of us now was to get to listen to that saved message, and then take it from there. I felt that with Matt coming to me that at least he had some doubt about my role in all of this and that the friendship still meant something to him.

"Okay, I will try not to overreact. I am going to tell you this once and once only, I didn't do it. I find it despicable that you would believe that in the first place. But go on, find this out for yourself and then let's take it from there. In the meantime, take responsibility for your actions and be a man about it. You started all this, it is no use looking for someone to blame. Blame yourself. Try and sort out this mess and take a long hard look at what you did. You are the one who couldn't keep it in your pants. Own up to it, confess. But I refuse to be your punching bag," I said to him.

A silent nod of the head was the only answer I received.

Matt then dropped me off and it was time to get ready for work as well. Everything would be fine, once the recording had been listened to, I would be absolved from all blame, and our friendship will return to normal again. This was certainly a test for our friendship, but one that I knew we would pass with distinction.

But doubt is cancerous and cantankerous. Albeit that Matt assured me that we were cool, brothers hanging together as always, I noticed a not so subtle change in Matt's behaviour towards me. We started spending less time together, his reasons being either he was working double shifts or he was going to make out with someone he met at the club, as Hilary still had not forgiven him and finally broke it off with him completely. This was serious, as the truth possibly would never come out now, as Hilary was the one with the recording, and there was no way she was prepared to let anyone listen to it as she had moved on with her life.

One evening I went to Matt's house again and he was getting ready to leave early for work again. Come around in the morning after work, I suggested to Matt, which usually was around three in the morning. But no, he needed to sleep, as he was tired, as night shift and double shifts were starting to get to him he said.

I know the signs of rejection, I felt and experienced the pangs before. Distant, cold, non-communicative. These were all the signals I received from my father, and I was on high alert. My bro. My best mate. He was starting to no longer value our friendship. Where I place a great value on friendship, I treasure it and will do everything possible to retain the friendship as far as possible, and believed Matt was similar in his approach to friendship, this, unfortunately, seemed like it was not to be.

One evening a tutoring lesson finished particularly late as it was exam time and the scholar and I had a lot of ground to cover to ensure that she was ready for the exam the following day. As I had no car in those days, I left work just after five in the afternoon, caught a bus at the local terminal in central town where I worked and got off at a bus station on Tranquillity's border around quarter to six in the evening. I then would dash to the scholar, where we would be busy until around half past six. This was our routine, Monday through Friday except for school holidays. On this evening, though, we only finished around eight o'clock. I walked the nine blocks home to our house, and as it was in the middle of winter, the wind howling and it being cold and dark, I walked with my head bowed, fighting the wind on my way home, towards warmth and sustenance. And to my surprise, whilst dancing and at times wrestling with the wind on my way home, I spotted Matt's vehicle at another of his friends' place. This is odd, I thought to myself, as Matt would have been working a double shift again. As I walked past this friend's house, Matt was just getting ready to leave, and he saw me walking past.

"Hop in," he said to me, "I will drop you off at home."

"Thanks, but I am fine. It is not too far to go still." I said.

"Don't be an ass, mate," Matt said. "I have taken the evening off. Let's roll."

"Let me get home first, eat, shower, change and then I will meet up with you later," I said. And so we agreed that Matt would pick me up in an hour's time, and we will shoot some pool in Brighton.

An hour later, the usual familiar sound of his car outside, and off to Brighton, we drove. Where in the past we would listen to music and I would sing to my heart's content, often irritating all in the vehicle but hardly ever giving a damn being carefree and jolly, or at times we would often have many different and serious conversations, on this particular evening, Matt was uncharacteristically quiet. And somehow, I just knew. The friendship and brotherhood that we had was no more. Matt believed still that I was the one who got him into trouble, and so like thawing ice in spring, he drifted away from our friendship.

"Matt," I said. "Let's give playing pool a skip. Let's drive around only. I am not in the mood for pool."

Matt nodded but said nothing.

"Matt," I continued, with heaviness in my heart that I never knew a grown man would feel. "I think there is something that you want to say to me. But you have been avoiding doing it."

Still, Matt said nothing. He kept on driving but said nothing.

"I think that we have reached the end of our friendship, Matt. I think you don't want this friendship any longer. I think you blame me for the breakup, you believe your mother and you believe that I wanted to see you unhappy.

"If that is the case, simply say it, drop me off at home, and we will go our separate ways, brother."

"Mate, you are right. I have been thinking about this long and hard and decided that I don't want to be friends with you any longer. It is best that way."

He turned the vehicle around and without any word further drove back home to drop me off and to move on with his life.

I showed no emotion during potentially one of the longest drives back to my place. I still said nothing as I got out of the car and walked into our house. Empty. Stripped bare. Abandoned. I lost my best friend, my true friend, my brother. Rejected by him for believing a tale that is yet to be proven as false and untrue. Cast aside, branded a traitor. That is how he ended our friendship. Maybe I wasn't a brother to him as he was to me, as after all, he had two other real blood brothers. Maybe, he had outgrown me. Maybe, who I was and am no longer was what he was looking for in a friend. And he surely blamed me for the breakup with Hilary.

Being rejected as a child was a tremendous ordeal, however, being rejected as an adult the pain knew no borders, had no boundaries. Alone. All alone. My best and only friend was gone. And then I started to cry. Sitting outside in the backyard, looking at the stars, a grown man, yet I cried, as I had not done for in a long time. The hole of rejection tore me apart. The hole in my soul caused a pain that I thought was so deeply buried and forgotten, but to my surprise it was a volcano, always just below the surface, waiting to erupt. Mom and Sis understood my emotions and left me to deal with it in the only way they knew I wanted to. Alone.

A few evenings later, there was a knock on our door. It was a Friday evening. I most definitely did not expect any company, so I was in my room, reading a book. Sis opened the door and called to me.

"Who is it?" I asked.

"Matt's mother." Was all that Sis said.

As I walked to the front door, Matt's mother has gotten back in her vehicle and called me to the side of her window.

"I am terribly sorry for what has happened between you and Matt," she said to me. "I never believed that anything could get between your friendship."

"But something did," I said to her. "And do you know what hurts the most?" I asked her.

She chose not to answer but continued to look at me and listened to what I had to say.

"The fact that you never even gave me the benefit of the doubt. I was like a child in your house. For more than six years. And when the time came to look for a scapegoat, you could look no further but me. That if you didn't believe it, you would have told

Matt from the start. The fact that you are here shows that even you believe that I had something to do with it."

I slowly turned around and walked quietly into the house, still hearing her car idling outside our house. Eventually, I heard the car drive off and I returned to reading my book. Tumultuous and tormented. But also strangely triumphant.

A few months later, one Sunday in church Phoebe came to me.

"Did you hear about Matt?" she asked me. "He found out who the person was who told Hillary those lies."

I shouldn't care, I told myself, but I still bloody did!

"What happened?" I couldn't stop myself from asking.

"My mother went to Hilary after all this time, although she is dating someone else. My mother told Hilary that Matt told her that he could not move on, that he had to know who the person was who phoned and left the message on her phone and managed to break up their relationship. After a long time of debating with my mother that she felt it was not the right thing to do, she finally agreed to tell Matt personally but only if he promised her that he would not confront the person who told her. And if he did, she would never ever contemplate being friends with him again. And when Matt contacted her, he promised to keep up his side of the agreement."

"Geez," I said, "he must have been mad once she told him who it was, but also glad that he knew who the hell meddled in his affairs."

"Not nearly as mad as when he found out that the person who ratted on him was our own cousin. Can you believe that? Roy. Because Roy fancied her and felt that Matt was not doing the right thing."

"What?"

"Yes, as you know, Roy and Matt never got along, and when Roy saw what Matt was doing he had no problem telling Hillary about the crap that he thought Matt was pulling. All those stupid lies."

"How did Matt react when he found out it was Roy?" I asked.

"He was enraged. But he still believes that there is a chance for him to get back with Hilary again, so, for now, he is going to live up to his promise."

"Geez, Phoebes," I said. "What a mess. Roy should have just let it be. You watch he will get what he deserves. The wheel turns. He has broken up a seemingly perfect relationship, and now Hilary is dating someone else, so in the end, he lost too."

Walking home from church that day, I felt nothing. No joy, no relief, nothing. No, I was mistaken. I felt emptiness, a void. A friendship came to an end because of one idiot. One jealous fool who coveted what he could and would never have and in the end destroyed three people's lives. Destroyed their enduring friend-ships and destroyed their relationships. And lost. And gained nothing. All of this for nothing. I did not condone Matt's actions, but I did not agree that for own personal gain, Roy interfered and told Hilary the truth.

A week later, Matt's mother came to me and asked me if I would consider being friends with Matt again.

"Did Matt send you?" I asked her.

"Of course not. He will be mad that I came to you in the first place," she said.

"Then why did you come and not him?"

"To make things right again. I could have intervened and stopped it all. I was wrong, I know that now. And I know how good friends the two of you were. And frankly, I don't like the new friends he is hanging out with."

A means to an end again, that is all that I am to her.

"How do I know that he still wants to be friends with me as well?" I asked her.

"He does. He has said to me on quite a few occasions losing the friendship is one of his biggest regrets."

"Ok," I said. "If this is truly what he wants, then tell Matt that if he also still wants to be friends with me that he needs to meet me at the hilltop of the primary school on Sunday afternoon at four. If he does not come, then I have my answer," I continued saying to her.

I then turned around and without saying goodbye or another word I walked into the house.

I never did go to the primary school hilltop that Sunday. And to this day, I do not know if Matt did go. I would like to believe that he did. But I could never be rejected by my brother again, and knowing how quickly the cards turned and how readily he believed that I was the one who failed him, I knew somewhere in the future again, something somehow will take place. And when it doesn't fit or doesn't make sense to them, and they would look for a scapegoat, I will be blamed. I could not be rejected by my best friend again for a second time, no matter what. Believe me, that Sunday was the hardest thing for me to do. To not go. To know this would be the final death throes of being rejected so many months ago. But as Shakespeare taught us in the Tempest, I will not rub the sore when in fact I should be bringing the plaster. A plaster that stayed on a festering sore for many years.

∗∗∗

As the floodgates of memories threatened to drown me, I decided that I had been cooped up for too long in the house this morning. That I would rather brave the rain and the cold and seek some companionship than spend the entire day reminiscing and analysing my soul and all the holes that punctured it. A dream and lyrics from a song. Was that really what had caused this tsunami of memories to hit me all at once? Or was there something deeper. I was not ready to psychoanalyse the deeper meaning and so I went downstairs. When I got to my car, I noticed that I did not take my wallet or my car keys, which is quite odd for me as I am very seldom if ever absentminded. Walking back up the stairs to my room, looking for my wallet and keys, my cell phone rang. Conversation at last.

"Hello?" I answered the phone, not recognising the number on my phone.

"Hi, there stranger." A voice from the past. Why now, what the hell is happening today, I thought to myself. Surely not this as well.

"I think you have the wrong number," I stated and abruptly ended the call. I sat down on my bed, thinking that voice, I would never forget that voice. And that voice albeit so silky at times was a voice that caused a flaming hole in my soul and almost ripped it apart.

3

THE HOLE OF BETRAYAL

*D*uring my years at university, I briefly dated Tania, and although this was one of my more serious relationships, I deeply cared about Tania, but after some time we simply drifted apart. And after Tania, I had a few casual flings but nothing that was serious enough that I felt I met the one true person that I would like to spend the rest of my life with. In between studies, later on work, tutoring lessons and friendships, there indeed was very little time for me to fall in love and meet the right girl on the one hand, and on the other hand, I never during this time met someone that I felt was the right one. I always believed and still believe that one will know when one has met *the* one and so I started to accept that this might very well be my lot in life: ambition, drive and loneliness.

After the friendship with Matt and us moving out of Tranquillity to another more affluent suburb in the west, I befriended a few work colleagues and from time to time, we would hang out together. I was wary of too involved friendships, as I still carried the scars of a friend's betrayal and loss. But as time went by, I eventually made friends with a lady who was fifteen years older than me. Linda stayed in the same suburb and street that we did, only a few houses from us and her vehicle happened to break down in front of our house the one morning as Linda was on her way to work.

Linda rang our front doorbell; surprised at such an early morning visit I went to open the door.

"Hi," Linda said to me. "Sorry to bother but I have been having trouble with my car."

"No bother at all. Do you need to phone someone to assist you?" I asked.

Linda was desperately in need of some help, but as I know nothing of cars I could only help if her battery was dead.

"No, no, not at all. I think maybe it is the battery. Could you perhaps assist me? I only live around the corner."

Fortunately, Linda's intuition was right as her vehicle only had a flat battery and I gladly assisted by jump-starting the vehicle so that she could get to work again. Linda was very thankful and explained that she would get the battery replaced the same day. That same evening, Linda knocked on our door and gave me a chocolate for helping a damsel in distress. Although I do not enjoy chocolates, I was not about to let Linda know that and invited her in. We chatted for a while and realised that we had a lot in common. And this became a start of a wonderful friendship. Linda was in need of a friend, and I fitted the profile.

So over time Linda and I would chat whenever we bumped into each other and the one day Linda invited me to dinner. I gladly accepted, as Linda was a refreshing distraction from an otherwise mundane existence, as I was busy building my career and continued with my tutoring lessons. Linda had two children, both in high school at the time and her husband had passed away several years before.

"I am a lonely person with not many friends. I am most certainly not looking for any serious relationship; I really was only in need of a friend, an escort and someone that I could trust." Linda confided in me.

Linda often had to go to work functions and detested going alone, as she believed that the other women with their husbands jealously guarded against any potential friendship with Linda and them. Not that she wanted it, but this is the sad reality of a single woman in her early forties. Unwittingly, Linda was unfairly seen as a cougar and hence had very few lady friends.

Gradually our friendship blossomed into true friendship, and I cared about Linda the way that one sibling cares about another. At the time that we became good friends, Linda and I both discussed what we wanted from the friendship and we both agreed that it would remain platonic between us. No strings attached, and only very good friends. At this junction in my life, I expressed a desire to go to Swakopmund in Namibia one day on holiday, and Linda secretly planned for us to have a vacation in Namibia. One evening while having dinner there again, Linda announced that the four of us would go on a road trip and the road trip included travelling through the vast landscapes of Namibia eventually to arrive at our destination in Swakopmund and its surrounding areas. I was extremely excited about going and a few weeks later, one Sunday morning, we set out in Linda's car on the way to the Namibian border for three blissful weeks.

Candice and James were as excited as this was not even school holidays, but somehow Linda managed to take them out of school for these three weeks.

Namibia was a blast. We stayed outside Swakopmund and rented a cottage with two bedrooms. James and I shared a bedroom and Linda and Candice shared one. As typical tourists, we went to all the different attractions and the weather in Swakopmund played along. Within a flash, the three weeks had flown by, and we returned home with our friendship intact and a bond between us that was considered very strange to have between a man and a woman, or so many of my other work friends and acquaintances told me.

Linda and I started to spend a lot of time together, and Saturday typically was set aside to go out for dinner and catch a movie. And we always had a lot of fun. Here we had a friendship that had no expectations other than to have a good time, to know someone both of us could rely on and to be there for one another. Our typical Saturday night would end with me dropping Linda off at home, making sure she was safe and then off to home I would go as well.

On one particular evening after watching a very good movie, Linda invited me to stay a while longer, to come in, as the children were out. I did not think anything of it, and as it was still relatively early, I followed Linda into the house. Linda went to the lounge and switched on a table lamp.

"Hey you," Linda said. "Would you like something to drink?"

"No thanks, I am still rather full after that great dinner and all the snacks we had during the movies."

I am very fond of singing, and Linda was as fond of listening to me sing, so she took out a CD, one that had many of my (our?) favourite songs, and I would sing along with the artist and Linda would listen and smile. But I sensed that something was different,

Linda's mood was strange and uncharacteristic and I could see where Linda wanted this to lead. But as my feelings for Linda had never developed beyond normal friendship, and we had a spoken agreement between us that we will not complicate our friendship, I was getting concerned that perhaps Linda did not keep up her side of the arrangement. But I could also be imagining things, I said to myself, trying to brush it off.

"Come, come dance with me?" Linda asked. This was the first time Linda ever asked me to dance outside of any work function that I would attend with her, but although I felt slightly uncomfortable, I took Linda in my arms and we danced a slow dance with REM singing about people getting hurt. Suddenly I became aware of Linda moving quite close up against me, I could feel the heat escaping from her.

"Linda," I whispered, "I don't think this is a good idea."

"Why not? We are alone and we are adults. I know what I am doing."

"Do you, Linda? Do you really?"

"Yes, I do, I want to feel wanted again," she murmured, still in my arms, still swaying to REM in the background. "Loved again, and to have a man love me again."

I slowly broke loose from the embrace, just as REM finished their song. I took a seat, watching Linda curling up on the couch opposite me, flushed and without any doubt quite angry.

"Linda, there is nothing more than I would like for you right now to have someone love you the way that you want them to. And trust me. I could make love to you now, right here. But this will unfortunately not change anything between us. We can always only be friends. And this will come and stand between us. Yes, I could make love to you right now, but this would be for all the wrong reasons. And I value our friendship too much to lose it over one silly evening of lust and desire. How would I be able to look you in the eye again after this one time? I love you and respect you too much to spoil the bond and friendship we have."

"So this is how you feel! That you would sleep with me but never love me," a dejected Linda sneered and burst out crying.

"No, Linda, this is not what I meant. I could never just use you and sleep with you, I care too much about you. But I refuse to give you hope. By making love to you, I am giving you hope that we will be more than friends and that we will progress from a friendship to a relationship. I know myself, Linda. I know how I feel about you. And I know that I could never love you in the way that you want me to love you. I am so sorry. If I have given you any reason to think otherwise, then please accept my apologies. I have never meant to send you any signals. More so, I have never meant to hurt you."

"I think it is better if you leave. I want to be alone," Linda said to me.

I didn't want to leave, but I realised that she needed to be by herself right then and that she felt humiliated by what happened. So I stood up, kissed her on the cheek and left quietly. And hated the fact that a wedge has been driven in between our friendship, a wedge that only Linda could cut down.

I decided to give Linda some time to think about our friendship; whether she could continue on a platonic basis only. So the following Friday evening I went over to Linda's. She opened the door after I rang the doorbell, and I could see both hurt and relief in her eyes at the same time.

"I think we need to talk, Linda," I started, but Linda interrupted me.

"It's not you. It's me. I have fallen for you and have loved you for a long time now. And in a different way than what you thought."

"Oh, Linda. I don't know what to say, as I did not see this one coming. And if this has been going on for a while now, I cannot imagine how difficult it must have been for you. If you feel it is better that we don't see each other anymore, I will fully understand and as difficult as it would be, I will have no alternative but to accept it."

I knew that it would hurt me if this was what Linda wanted, but I would have sacrificed our friendship readily if it meant that I would not hurt Linda any more than what she has gone through already. I cared too much about her and her well-being than staying friends and in the meantime, she pines away and is in misery.

"No, oh heavens, no!" Linda cried out.

"I have managed to live with how I feel for a long time now, and it did not change our friendship. I had a relapse, a moment of weakness. Please don't let this change our friendship. I'll rather have a piece of you than nothing at all. I will learn to cope with it and come to accept this over time. All that I need is time."

It broke my heart. Dear Lord, I prayed, forgive me for this was never what I wanted for Linda. I hugged Linda and consoled her, and when she started to cry, I cried with her. A while later, I kissed her on the cheek and left and went home with the promise of going to dinner and a movie the next evening. I felt desolate. How could I have not seen the signs? How could I have not noticed a change in her behaviour? How am I going to continue our friendship without hurting her?

Knowing what I knew, I also knew there was no way that I was going to desert Linda. I was going to be careful not to encourage her feelings for me and to make sure, without hurting her that our friendship is platonic and that we could never move beyond that.

The next evening we went to dinner again as planned, and although it started off awkwardly, we managed to overcome the awkwardness and just be ourselves again with only a tiny bit of discomfort that we both worked very hard at to overcome and ignore. And we never referred to what happened that evening again. I knew that Linda's feelings for me never changed, if anything, it got deeper. But my heart could not turn friendship into love, no matter how much I tried. And I would not ever turn my back on our friendship unless Linda asked me to.

One Saturday evening a few months later I was invited to a barbecue at a work colleague and friend's house. I asked Linda if we could skip our routine, as these were some good friends I made at work, and Linda had no problem with me going to the barbecue.

I arrived slightly late, and my friends took me through to where the rest of their friends and colleagues, some mutual some not, were mingling and enjoying the evening. Then I saw her. Zoe. Zoe, with the long blonde hair and piercing blue eyes. Drop dead gorgeous, with a tiny waist and beautifully tanned legs. In a flash, without a single doubt, I completely lost my heart. I always believed that love, at first sight, is for fairy tales and love stories. It doesn't happen in real life. But here I was. My mouth was dry, my heart was racing, my mind was in turmoil, and all I could do was stare. Stare at the most wonderful, extravagant, out of this world, stunning and beautiful being I have ever laid my eyes on.

"Not in your class, laddie!" I reminded and reprimanded myself. But too late. I completely lost it. Without her even saying a single word. I mustered all the confidence I had and floated towards her. Zoe was standing all alone to the one side.

"You look as lost as I feel," I croaked.

She smiled at me, and right there I died a thousand deaths.

"Hi," I managed to say, less croaky than before then stumbled while introducing myself.

"Zoe," she huskily introduced herself to me.

"Do you know all these people?" I asked her.

"Hardly," she said. "Carole and John are the only people I know. And now you."

We immediately hit it off, and for the rest of the evening, we were inseparable. For Zoe, I think the reason was that she felt like a stranger not knowing everyone, but for me, it was that I immediately knew that I have found the right one. I simply could not let her go. Surprisingly, Zoe was easy to talk to, enjoyed my warped sense of humour and in fact, I felt she enjoyed the time with me. We were the last ones to leave the barbecue that evening, and as it was very late in the evening, I offered to follow Zoe home to make sure that she would arrive there safe and sound. Zoe protested, but I did not want to hear anything about it, convincing her that it was the gentlemanly thing to do.

So I followed Zoe to where she stayed, she opened the gates of the townhouse complex she lived in and spoke to the guards, letting them know that I was a guest. When she parked her vehicle in her garage, she showed me the visitor's parking bay, and we continued talking for a few more minutes. I was absolutely infatuated by Zoe, loved her from the first moment and did not want this evening to end.

"Thank you, for bringing me home and making sure that I am alright."

"Zoe," I murmured, "I know this is inappropriate. But there is one thing that I would very much like to do."

"And what is that, mister?" she asked with a twinkle in her eye.

"I really would like to kiss you."

"So what are you waiting for?" she whispered. I slowly leant forward and then kissed her lips. Touching her lips and tasting her sweet breath, exquisite.

After a while, we pulled apart. I was flushed. Flying, soaring, no longer floating. Thank you, Lord, I still managed in my delirious state.

"Listen, you are a sweet guy," Zoe began.

Oh no, I thought, the dreaded turndown, the dreaded you are not the one for me. Torture, pure and utter torture.

"I have just broken up with someone after a two year relationship. I am on the rebound and I still hurt. I don't want to give you any false hope, as I have none right now. I am not ready for a relationship."

"Zoe, I fully understand," I said. "What I am going to do is give you my number. When you want to see me again, give me a call, and I will be here. But call me. This can be the start of something wonderful. If you allow it to. And I will take it slow. I promise."

"Take my number as well. In case I do not call, maybe I am down, and maybe you will cheer me up."

So we both exchanged numbers, and I left elated. This was a start. Granted, we did not hit it off the way I wanted it to happen despite the kiss, but I loved her. Plain and simple. I could not explain it, but I knew it. Without a shadow of a doubt, I had met my soulmate. And she had beguiled me like no other.

Driving home was the worst and the best for me. Worst as I had to leave Zoe behind and best as I had never known what it was to truly love someone this way. And I know it sounds ludicrous, to some even preposterous, but it is not. I loved her from the moment I saw her. I knew that if I was to pursue this, that Linda had to know, and that I will still make the friendship work between us. Linda is as much a part of my life as I would like Zoe to become. And I hoped and prayed that if anything blossomed between me and Zoe, that Linda would remain friends with me and possibly with Zoe as well. I knew I was naive and that this would probably never happen, but I had to give it a shot, as on the one hand, I loved my true friend and on the other hand, I met my soulmate, the love of my life.

The Monday morning at work, my staff members sensed a change. And Melody, my most loyal soldier who reported to me, and with whom I had a special bond, I decided to confide in her.

"I met someone on Saturday evening," I said to her.

"Ooh, la la. I can see it. Your head is up in the clouds," she said.

"Melody, this is the one. She, unfortunately, has just broken up with her boyfriend of two years, she is on the rebound and may very well still take him back. But I just know. She is the one. I gave her my number and told her I will not be a nuisance, that when she is ready, she can contact me. She also gave me her number."

"Give her time, my friend. When she is ready, and if she was attracted to you, and there is no chance of her getting back together with her boyfriend, then she will call. There is also hope as she shared her number with you. So you will have to be patient, and this is not one of your stronger suits."

"There are too many 'ifs' in all of that," I complained. Melody merely laughed. And that Monday dragged on, but no call from Zoe.

Tuesday, I was restless. I knew that this was too soon but also wanted her so much to call. I prayed and asked the Lord that if she is the right one, please let her call. Tuesday ended, with not a single call from her.

Wednesday was a busy day, but I had my phone with me the whole time, and again, no missed call, no voicemail, no Zoe. By this time, I was bursting at the seams with impatience.

"I am going to give her a call," I said to Melody. "First thing tomorrow morning."

Melody said nothing, with a knowing look in her eyes.

Thursday morning I had a few meetings to attend, and close to lunchtime, I had time to give Zoe a call. With shaking hands, I dialled her number. And got voicemail! The phone did not ring, went straight to voicemail.

"Hi," I said. "It is me. I was thinking about you and hope that you are okay. Chat soon again."

This was all that I managed to say. The day ended, and no returned voicemail from Zoe.

Friday also went by without a single call, and Melody could see that I was starting to get despondent. Sure, I understood that Zoe was not ready for something serious, she had just been in a relationship and was on the rebound. But surely she felt the connection. And that we could start off as friends. Even if it did not work out as lovers, we then still could have had each other. I would love her with everything in me, even if it was unrequited as long as I could have her in my life. That was what I was coveting with every fibre of my being.

"My dear boss and friend," Melody said. "Perhaps she is not ready for the next step in her life. You have made the first move. Now give her time. Let things run its course. You are too impatient. Take your time. If it is meant to be, Zoe will contact you."

I spent the weekend pretended to be in a frivolous mood, albeit only on the surface. Deep down I was hoping and praying that I would be able to get to know my soulmate better. Linda and I went to dinner and a movie again, and although I was trying hard to be pleasant, Linda noticed my mood.

"Your eyes are not smiling with the rest of you," Linda remarked. "Is something the matter?"

"No, Linda, I only have a few things on my mind. Sorry if I am a bit of a pain right now."

So the weekend went by, uneventful, and I was starting to believe that Zoe was not meant to be. The Monday morning at work, I was quite busy in meetings and had a few missed calls on my cellular phone. I did not recognise the one particular number, but once I listened to the voicemail messages; my heart did a double somersault.

"Hey, you. This is Zoe. I don't know if you have been trying to get in contact with me, but I had to change numbers as my ex was stalking me. This is my new number. Please call me when you have a moment."

With hands shaking so badly, I dialled the number only to get the operator telling me the number does not exist. I dialled the number again, and the best sound ever was resounding in my ear, the sound of a phone ringing. Zoe answered it on the third ring.

"Hi, Zoe, it is me."

"Hello! What a nice surprise. Thank you for calling me back."

"I tried calling you last week, and left a message but guess you didn't get it because you have changed numbers?"

"Yes. Michael is being a dick, so the only way for him to stop harassing me was for me to change my number. You say that you called me?"

"I did, on Thursday. So…" I said.

"So…" Zoe echoed.

"Are you busy tonight? Can I come over and can we spend some time together?"

"Can we make it for tomorrow evening?" Zoe asked. "I will make us dinner."

This became the start of a friendship. For me a love affair, but as Zoe was hurt and on the rebound, it was best to look at it as a friendship, I reasoned with myself. That Tuesday was the best time ever, we laughed a lot, had an easy way of talking about anything, and when listening to music we were comfortable in each other's presence, with no need of conversing the whole time. Being together was enough. Spending time together and getting to know one another were bonuses. And, at the end of the evening, I had to see Zoe again.

"So, when will I be able to see you again?" I asked.

"When would you like to see me again?" Zoe asked coyly.

We agreed that we would spend time together the coming Thursday and Friday. I did not commit to Saturdays, as I knew that this was the time with Linda, and I also knew that I had to explain this to Zoe.

A few weeks later, after spending Tuesdays, Thursdays and Fridays together, I felt that I needed to explain my absence on Saturdays to Zoe. Although Zoe never asked, I knew she was puzzled at the fact that we did not spend Saturdays together.

"Zoe, listen," I started. "There is something I need to tell you."

"Please don't tell me that you have someone in your life!" Zoe looked at me with scared doe eyes.

"Zoe. I do not have a girlfriend in the true sense of the word," I started off and then I explained to Zoe the special bond of friendship Linda and I had. I assured Zoe that it was platonic, that Linda has been a friend for many years, has been there for me during very tough times, and that I treasured our friendship.

"I want to continue seeing you, Zoe. And I hope that we could one day progress beyond just being friends. But I need you to understand that Linda is a part of my life and she is a very special friend to me. Please allow me this friendship, and know very well that if it could have been more than friendship, it would have been so a very long time ago. It is not and will not be. But I cannot and will not turn my back on Linda."

Zoe was sceptical, but I sensed that the friendship was as important to her, so she agreed to give it a shot.

"Promise me one thing," Zoe said with urgency. "Promise me that you will never hurt me. Not now not ever. I know we are only friends now, but you said it yourself, maybe we can grow into a relationship. I have been hurt terribly and I am scared of going into a relationship."

"Zoe, I promise you. I will never hurt you. I will never break your heart."

With Zoe in my life, people started seeing a change in me. Somehow people could see that I was in love. This did not escape Linda either. Linda did not pry, did not ask, and I realised that the time had come that I needed Linda to understand that I met someone, but that our friendship will not suffer because of it. I knew how Linda felt and was afraid of hurting her, but by not telling her, I was going to hurt her even more. I knew that we simply had to find a way for this to work as I loved Linda dearly and would do everything in my power to keep our friendship alive.

"Linda. You and I have been friends for many years now. And we have always only been honest with each other. A few weeks ago, I met someone, and I have fallen in love with her."

Linda went all pale, ashen looking. Bewildered even. I could see that Linda was somehow expecting this and at the same time had hoped that it would not happen. That it would not be real.

"I told her about you. I told her that we are very good friends and that our friendship remains one of the most important things to me in my life. And that I was not prepared to give up on our friendship. That I would never do that to you, or me."

Linda was at a loss for words and did not respond to what I was telling her immediately. I realised that she must have had a thousand thoughts and million things going through her mind right then.

"Saturdays will remain ours. We will still go to movies and still have dinner," I went on, trying to gauge how Linda was reacting to what I just said. But Linda said nothing. She just nodded her head the whole time. Eventually, after a long while, Linda asked me if I would mind to leave her alone, as she had a lot on her mind and a lot to think about. I knew it would be selfish of me to try and rationalise with her, as Linda had to work this out. I truly hoped that she would want to continue with our friendship, as I did not want to lose her at all. She was there through many trying times and I wanted her to be happy for me, with me and continue being a part of my life. But I was also realistic enough to know that I could not force this acceptance upon her, that Linda had to decide whether she could continue on this basis, or whether it was best for her to simply walk away.

A few days later, Linda called me and said she wanted to see me. I went over to her house, so desperately hoping that this could work out well for all of us.

"Please don't interrupt me. I can only say this once, so let me finish. I do not know if I could continue with our friendship, as despite what we agreed upon, my feelings for you have never changed. And I could live with it while I had all of you, or most of you at least. Now I need to share you. And I will have less of you. And the one thing that I always hoped I would get from you, I now know I will never get. That hurts. I know, no one is to blame here. I did not ask to fall in love with you, or to love you the way I do. I just did. And I just do. I cannot change that. I cannot change the fact that you will never love me the way I want you to. I cannot change the fact that you love another in a way I always hoped and prayed one day you would love me. But, I am willing to give this a try. But be warned: I will walk away if the pain and hurt become unbearable. And I do not ever want to know about the two of you, don't talk about her and don't talk about your relationship. Those are my terms. That is the only way I could possibly, and I say possibly strongly here, that I could cope with this."

Linda looked so distraught, so unhappy that I hated myself at that moment. Hated myself for not being able to love her, for hurting her without even trying to hurt her. Asking myself if I was being selfish for wanting both of them in my life, as I loved them both in different ways. But I promised myself that I would as far as possible protect her and what we have. And knew that I had a balancing act awaiting me, but one that I simply had to make work.

117

So for the next few months, I would spend my Tuesdays, Thursdays and Fridays with Zoe, and Saturdays with Linda. I could not sense any change in Linda's behaviour and desperately wanted to believe that she accepted that I had someone in my life and that I still valued her as a true and loyal friend. Zoe also early on came to the conclusion that I would never betray her, that everything I said was true, and our friendship really started to blossom into something more. I loved her with all my heart and slowly I saw the change in her. Little things. The excitement of greeting me, the anticipation before a kiss, and the blushing scarlet of her cheeks during candle-lit dinners. Gradually, Zoe was getting over her previous failed relationship and started to fall in love with me. I was head over heels for all the time I knew her, and also came to the realisation that over time and with patience Zoe would also fall in love with me. We practically became inseparable. On the days that we did not see each other we would spend long hours on the phone, talking and loving the sound of each other's voices, enjoying each and every of our conversations.

As time kept on moving along, I wanted to spend more and more time with Zoe. Eventually, I started seeing Zoe on Sundays as well, but I realised that Saturdays were also a need. But Linda remained a priority for me, so I had to find a compromise. So after almost a year of seeing Linda every Saturday, and the rest of the time spending it with Zoe, except for Mondays, Wednesdays and Saturdays, I felt a hunger in me to see more of Zoe, be more with her. I could no longer be satisfied with the time that we spent together. So one Saturday evening after dinner and a movie with Linda, I tried to break it to her gently.

"Linda, it has been over a year now since I have met Zoe. And in all this time, our friendship remained intact," I started. "But my relationship with Zoe is at a stage where I have a need to see more of her. So I was thinking of how best to do this without taking time away from you and me. If you agree to what I have in mind, I believe this could work well for us?"

Linda looked at me, and for a startled second or two, I thought I saw disdain and contempt in her eyes. But Linda said nothing, looking at me as if she was expecting the worst.

"If you are in agreement, I would like me and you to go to the Saturday afternoon show and no longer the evening show. I also thought of us having dinner on Wednesday evening, so I will pick you up after work, and we will go for dinner. This way, we will still have dinner together, but no longer on Saturday evenings."

Again, I saw the pain in Linda's eyes, together with a look of scorn, even hate. The one thing I never wanted to do was happening right in front of me: I was hurting the one person I promised I never would. No matter what justification is used, I continued our friendship knowing that here was a woman who loved me and would do anything possible to keep me in her life. I felt desolate and lost. On the one hand, I needed more time with Zoe, but on the other hand, this should never be at the expense of Linda.

"I have a better idea," Linda said after a while. "I will cook for us on Wednesday evenings. This way, we can spend time at home with the kids, if they are not out with friends. I am tired after work and would not be very good company if we had to go out still. As I need to cook in any case, please come over for dinner then every Wednesday evening."

I knew Linda accepted this offer, more because she realised that it still meant that we could spend time together and less about the fact that she was resigned to accepting the new arrangement.

And so, Zoe and I also had Saturday evenings for and to ourselves. Linda and I watched the five o'clock show and after the movie, I would drop Linda off, sometimes going in to have a cold drink, other times just walking Linda to the door. I then would drive to Zoe's where I would spend the rest of the evening before returning home early in the morning. Sis would open the gates for me, as she waited for my call when I left Zoe's so that she would know what time I would be home. Sis was very protective over me and me over her, so this was an arrangement that suited both of us when we went out and had to wait for the other to return home.

Zoe and I were really starting to get close, and I hoped that Zoe was ready to take our relationship to the next level. I had wanted her for a very long time, and I restrained myself from showing her how I felt on several occasions, as I wanted our first time to be special and exquisite. I was under no disillusion of Zoe's virginity, as she and her ex had lived together before their breakup, so this most certainly would not be her first time. And it would also not be mine. But because I loved her with everything that I had in me, and with Zoe being my soulmate, I knew that our first time together would be amazing.

So the one Saturday evening, after a candlelit dinner, we started kissing, and I recognised a hunger in Zoe's kisses. Emboldened by her fierce kisses and murmurs, I started caressing Zoe in a different and more seductive way, and her responsiveness urged and turned me on. Touching Zoe in an intimate way was what I had been dreaming of for a long time, but somehow I was not ready for the sweet moment of truth. With shaking hands, I started touching her secret places, reserved only for the very special. When she cried out when I explored her sweet hidden crevice, my whole body was electrified. Every hair stood erected. I have never been so aware of the musky odours of another person so close as only two true lovers can be. With my hands, my mouth and my tongue, I explored her body, getting to know her body so well, what worked for her, what excited her, what made her catch her breath. Finally, when two lovers come together as one in a silent rhythm that only they dance to, to their own seductive music, knowing each move will take you higher to more ecstasy, there was no turning back from this sweet and fulfilling moment. Crying out in release, spent and yet hesitant to withdraw, we finally collapsed in a breathless tumble, realising that we just made our two worlds collide in a shattering force of delight.

Words were not needed to describe what we have just experienced. And we kept at it for several times thereafter. And this newfound joy in our relationship just built on the blocks that were already laid and cemented together. From here on onwards, our relationship would be stronger and we would love each other, make love to each other, and enjoy the company of each other as only two lovers can do.

One night after making love again, with Zoe in my arms, I was caressing her hair while she was on the brink of sleep. And when I heard a soft snoring sound coming from her, I kissed her lightly on the mouth. "I love you, Zoe," I whispered. "I loved you from the first night I met you." Saying those words aloud, although Zoe was asleep was the ultimate confession to me. And it felt so right. Nothing felt more right. Having her in my arms, the taste of her on my lips, her sleeping next to me, in my willing arms and telling her I loved her. Loved her from the day I saw her.

Then she softly whispered to me, talking in her sleep, "I love you, too."

My heart skipped a beat. We had never used the "L" word before, not in any conversation. I said it aloud, what were the odds that Zoe would say the words in her sleep? The realisation that she felt the same way about me brought a deep sense of happiness, elation and satisfaction over me. The love of my life, my soulmate loves me as well. Affirmed love, endless love, blissful love.

I never mentioned to Zoe that I heard her speaking in her sleep, and as she did not refer to the conversation I had with her while she was sleeping, I felt that I needed to say it to her at the right time. The next Saturday we went out for dinner, and over candlelight and soft music in the background, I knew this was the right time, the perfect setting for telling Zoe how I felt.

"Zoe," I started. "We have been spending a lot of time together and we have been friends now for a long time and recently also became lovers. I have been enjoying every moment that I spend with you. I know that you got hurt in the past, and from time to time, I can still see the hurt in your eyes. But I will never hurt you. Zoe, I love you. I loved you the first time I laid eyes on you. I will always love you and want to spend as much time with you."

"Oh," Zoe started to cry.

Somehow, I knew these were tears of happiness and not of sadness. I started to cry with her, as I could never have known that one person could have such overwhelming feelings for another. I took her in my arms and slowly rocked her.

"I love you too," Zoe confirmed. We kissed and through our tears of happiness, we both realised that we just crossed a line that there is no turning back from. But neither of us wanted to turn around. What we had and what we shared was beautiful, precious and a special bond between two people that loved each other despite knowing their shortcomings. And knew that this was only the start and that so much love, laughter, pleasure and happiness awaited us as we continued to spend every possible moment together.

As our relationship became deeper, and my love for Zoe became more intense, I noticed at first a subtle change in Linda's behaviour. I continued my Wednesday evening dinners at Linda's place, and Saturday afternoon movies, but Linda became less and less interested in spending more time with me than was necessary. On Wednesday evenings after dinner, we usually would sit and chat for a while on anything other than Zoe and I would leave just before nine o'clock as it was a work night. However, Linda became antsy and I could see in her behaviour that she wanted me to leave after we had dinner and that there was no need to stay and chat.

I obliged, leaving early, and noticed relief on Linda's face when I mentioned that I was leaving. This seemed to be quite odd behaviour, but initially, I believed that Linda was perhaps only tired. However, Linda's behaviour became increasingly odd, to the point that I needed to understand what was going on. She even from time to time requested that we no longer go to the movies, that if I felt like it I could come over for an hour or so, but not longer as she was tired or wanted to do something and therefore wanted an early evening. Linda still meant the world to me and I still valued our friendship very much, so I was dumbfounded at her reaction. As I did not see it getting any better, in fact, I saw it getting worse and worse in that Linda had less of a need to spend time with me. One Wednesday evening after dinner, I decided that it was time to talk to Linda to find out what has been troubling her mind and why she was acting so distantly.

"Linda," I started. "For a while now I have noticed that something has been amiss. There is a change in your behaviour and I do not know if it is something that I have done."

"Not now, I am tired and want to get to bed early."

"I understand, Linda. But I also need to understand what has been upsetting you so that it causes you to want to spend less and less time with me."

"Why do you always think it is about you?" Linda snapped.

"Life does not revolve around you. Have you perhaps stopped for a moment and think that it was about me and not self-centred you?"

Those words that Linda flung at me hurt like a scorching metal. This was completely irrational behaviour from my best friend. I cared about our friendship and wanted to ensure that it remains intact for as long as possible. I even hoped that one day Linda and Zoe would become friends, as I hoped against all hopes that I could make it work one day.

"I am sorry, Linda," I uttered an apology. "I just wanted to make sure that you were fine and that everything was well with you. And yes, with us and our friendship."

"Oh, get off your high horse!" Linda yelled at me. "Open your damn eyes and see what has been going on for a while now."

"What, Linda? What has been going on?" I asked, getting angry at her response but telling myself that I needed to stay calm, as our friendship remained a treasure to me that I could not lose and did not want to give up at any cost.

"Do I have to shout it out to you?" Linda continued yelling.

"Yes, damn it, tell me!" I yelled back at her.

"You forced me away from you, pushed me away from you. You made me believe that I was only good enough to get your leftovers. Dinner and a movie. You always knew how I felt about you, but you never were man enough to give up on me. For your own selfish reasons. And through all this you allowed me to get hurt. To get hurt every time I saw you. Every single damned time we spent together, I was reminded that I was not good enough for you. That you could never love me the way I wanted you to."

"For heaven sake! You knew from day one how I felt and you knew and agreed to us only being friends. Why did you agree to it if it hurt you every time? Why did you not put an end to it?"

"Because I loved you. And the foolish woman that I am, I thought that you would grow to love me one day. That I only needed to be patient. Then you met that slut. And I knew that I could never have you the way she had. And that pushed me away from you."

"Listen here, Linda, you don't know Zoe so I will allow you this one time to insult her, but never again."

"Or what? Are you going to walk out on our friendship? Breaking news! I am walking out on it. I am. I have finally met someone who loves me for me. For me, don't you get it? Can you understand that? Someone who is not scared to love me and make love to me. Someone who cares about me and who has finally made me see what you are and what you have done to my life. And that it has always only ever been about you and your needs. Well, no more. No, more, as I had enough. It ends tonight. After tonight, I never want to see you again. Ever. After tonight, you are dead to me. You have almost destroyed me. I was too blind to see it. But now I do. And I love again, thank God. I finally love again." Linda broke down and sobbed.

I silently stood up, took my car keys from the kitchen counter top, walked out the door, climbed in my car and drove home. Willing the drive to end, as I refused to think about what just happened. I needed time alone to process what just happened, and did not feel like doing it while driving. But while driving home, I realised that once again, I lost a true friend.

The drive home, which usually is only a five-minute drive, felt like an eternity. When I did arrive home, Sis realised that something was wrong, but I was not ready to talk about it to anyone. I took a shower and went into my room, thinking about the things that Linda said when my cell phone rang. I so hoped it was Linda, but saw that it was Zoe.

"Hallo, baby," Zoe said on the other side of the phone.

"Hi, my angel," I said.

"What's wrong, baby? I can hear it in your voice."

"I am just tired, my love. Rather tell me about your day?"

"No, my love. I know you too well. I sense that something is wrong. Talk to me damn it. Share with me what is going on."

"Linda just chased me away and ended our friendship," I answered Zoe, saying the dreaded words out loud that have been mulling in my mind since I arrived home.

"What?" Zoe gasped. "My poor baby. Oh, I am so sorry, baby. Why don't you come over now and we talk about it?"

I got dressed again and drove over to Zoe's and we talked for hours. I told her everything Linda said to me, and Zoe just listened. I tried to rationalise, defend and justify my friendship with Linda, wanting Zoe to understand that it was never my intention to hurt Linda, yet that was all I ever did. From the first time, I rejected her advances and continued staying friends with her. I was heartbroken. Friendship to me has always been very important and I loved Linda very much. Losing her was one of the hardest things I ever had to endure, and that evening, with Zoe by my side, I cried. I cried for all the hurt in this world, for the injustice and for the unfairness. I cried for unrequited love and for misunderstandings. I cried for losses, losing loved ones and dear ones, Linda who was a part of my life for such a long time and who in her own way defined me. And through all this, Zoe merely listened, as she knew that words would be superfluous. She knew also that the only encouragement I needed and craved was to have her near me, to be able to share my feelings and to show how I felt about losing one of my best friends ever. After all the talking, I finally left in the early hours of the morning going back home, as I needed to wake up later on that morning for work. And as I was driving home, my soul had an empty feeling, as if something that was part of my soul for such a long time has been detached, ripped away even and has moved on and away. Leaving a wound on my soul that would take a very long time to heal. Sure, I was glad that Linda finally met someone, but I was saddened that it took place at the expense of our friendship. That Linda could not make the same sacrifice as I did. That Linda was not prepared to have a lover on the one hand and a friend on the other hand. That she could not have imagined the four of us spending time together and remaining friends, and creating new friendship bonds. I realised also that the hurt that I caused her brought her some kind of happiness in the end, but at my expense. That perhaps this was the price I had to pay for what I did to her. Retribution. Although all I ever wanted for Linda was happiness, and for us to be friends. This, however, was not enough for her. And the only way forward for Linda was out.

The first few months without the routine of visiting Linda was enormously difficult, at times I was sad, other times I was angry, and at other times I was at peace knowing that Linda was finally being loved the way she deserved. For a long time, I did not see Linda but continued thinking about her, hoping that one day she would understand what she meant to me. And deep down I hoped that she regretted throwing our friendship away, walking away from it and giving it up the way she did. But then again I reprimanded myself, telling myself that this was perhaps her atonement. That she had to walk away from it to be free from it and to be free to love somebody else.

It took me more than a year to get used to the idea that Wednesday evenings were spent at home and that Saturday movies were a thing of the past. Zoe and I kept to our arrangement that Mondays and Wednesdays were our days away from each other, as we both believed that this absence would make us appreciate each other and our relationship so much more. And this indeed was the case. Not seeing each other twice a week was made up for during the rest of the time, and I finally started spending the entire evening with Zoe over weekends, no longer leaving in the early hours of the morning. Weekdays were workdays and therefore, I left at a reasonable hour for both of us, if we could manage to break free from our embraces or cuddles. Zoe was the love of my life, and with spending time with her, slowly the ache of losing Linda morphed into a dull pain. I would never forget Linda, but with Zoe by my side, I had no choice and all the reason but to move on. Life goes on. Linda has moved on, and there was nothing more that I could do about it.

Spending our third year together, Zoe and I started making plans on moving in together. Although our Mondays and Wednesdays were spent apart as we decided early on, we also realised that our relationship has reached a new level and that progressively the next step would be to move in together. Zoe's parents would not necessarily agree to this, as they always wanted me to do the right thing and make an honest lady out of her. But Zoe and I had other plans. Whilst thinking about the best way of moving in together, talking about all the options that were available to us, I gradually started to see a change in Zoe's excitement of us moving in together. I initially thought that her parents again were standing in the way.

"Zoe, is something bothering you about us moving in together? Is it your dad again?" I asked her one evening.

"No, my love, it is not Dad. I think that we are maybe moving too fast right now?"

Too fast? How is this possible? I have spent every weekend at her place, sleeping over, we were lovers, we were intimate, and we were best friends. How can the next logical step be moving too fast?

"What do you mean, we are moving too fast? We have been together for three years now, we love each other and I thought that you as much as I wanted us to spend every moment that we have together. So what has changed?" I wanted to understand this sudden change in mood.

"Nothing has changed. I think we must just give it a bit more time. Moving in together is a huge step for me, for us, and for my parents, although they are not my primary concern right now. I just think we need to wait a few more months and see if the need to move in together is still there."

"Why would it not?"

"I am not saying it will not!" an exasperated Zoe answered me. "I am saying, give me time. That's all I am asking."

This behaviour seemed odd to me, as we have been talking about moving in together for quite some time, and this sudden turn of events was totally beyond me. But I loved Zoe and I was not going to rush her into something, only for both of us to regret it later on. So for a while, I decided to cool down on the discussions around moving in together. But Zoe's mood did not ease, her restlessness was constant, and I simply could not get through to her to understand this sudden change in behaviour. We still laughed and cooked together, making love was as awesome as it always was and there was no tangible change in the way we behaved with one another. But there was a broodiness and moodiness around Zoe that I simply could not explain.

One Tuesday evening as I was visiting, I noticed that Zoe was withdrawn. She only responded when required to do so during the conversation, and this particular evening she did not feel like making love. This was the first, as Zoe usually enjoyed our making out and being intimate but I also had it lucky for the last few years in that Zoe was always game and always in the mood. So I did not make a big deal out of it, I simply held her in my arms and we watched a movie together before I left and went home. Kissing her goodbye felt no different than any other evening, so I decided that Zoe was merely tired and had a lot on her mind. I have learned not to pry, Zoe would reveal at the right time when she was ready to talk about what was on her mind.

The Wednesday at work I tried to call her but she was not available to take my calls at all during the day. This was indeed odd, I thought to myself. First, she did not want to make love, and now she was not taking my calls. Clearly, something was wrong and Zoe's behaviour was quite odd. So I decided that I would after dinner at home that evening, pop in at Zoe's to see whether she wanted to talk about what was troubling her mind. I decided not to tell her that I was coming over, as she probably would protest and try to dissuade me from coming over. I needed to understand why my soulmate was troubled and how I could make it right again. I drove over to Zoe's a little after seven o'clock that evening, and as I entered the gated complex, to which by now I had a remote for, I noticed that Zoe's car was parked in its usual place. So at least Zoe was at home and not out with friends, which happened from time to time. I also had a key to the townhouse, so I could let myself in at any given time if so required. As I walked towards her townhouse, I noticed that the front was all dark. Could she be sleeping? Is she sick perhaps? I rushed to the door, took out the key, turned the key, opened the door, and stepped into the townhouse. I faintly heard some background music playing, coming from Zoe's bedroom. Afraid to wake her in case she was sleeping as a result of her being ill, I tiptoed to her bedroom. The door was not closed completely and stood slightly ajar. When I pushed the door open and looked into Zoe's bedroom, dim light from her bedside lamp was the only light in the room. But what I saw happening in front of me my mind, first of all, did not and could not register. It took me a few minutes to realise exactly what I was seeing, and my soul broke and shattered in thousand pieces. Zoe was murmuring and moaning in ecstasy, as she was in bed fornicating with some other man. My first instinct was to rush at the man and beat the living daylights out of him but realised that it would be a foolish thing to do. Zoe was as much at fault here, and who knows what lies she had been feeding this man.

"Just what the hell do you think you are doing, Zoe!" I shouted at her. In a flash, all erotic thoughts and actions came to an end as Zoe grabbed for the light. Her partner tried to cover himself.

"Who the hell are you?" he asked me.

"Get out. Get out or else I will throw your sorry ass out of here. You are in bed with my girlfriend. Get out now while I am still sane. But I will not ask you again," I whispered to the man.

It must have been something in the way I said it that gave him pause and he realised that he had to get out of there very quickly. He fumbled for his clothes, moving very quickly passed me and out the door. I heard him close the front door on his way out. All this time, all that I could do was look at Zoe, with shock, dismay, loathing, anger, hatred and sorrow. The one person whom I have loved with all my heart and soul, unconditionally loved, loved and beguiled the first time I ever laid eyes on her, could not have hurt me more in life other than through this absolute betrayal. Bitter words burned on my tongue but were never uttered, staying behind choked in my mouth. I wanted to tear her world apart the way she had torn my world and soul apart but only looked at her. A million thoughts ran through my mind, things I needed to say, wanted to say, wanted to call her, wanted to accuse her of. All of it dying on my burning tongue before I uttered a word.

After standing like that, which felt like an eternity, I simply asked one question, "Why, Zoe?"

Ashamed, caught in the act, caught out, frightened I supposed, Zoe could not really answer me immediately. She slowly got out of bed, started to get dressed and looked at me as if it were the first time she laid eyes on me.

Zoe started, "I think it is best if you leave now. I don't want to talk about what just happened. Not now. Maybe later. But not now. Please. I ask you, please, I need you to leave. Go now."

I realised then that if I insisted on staying, if I tried to get her to tell me why she did what she did, that I would lose her forever. I was not sure that I still wanted her after what she has done, but if there was even a remote chance of us getting through this terrible, soul-destroying ordeal, then it was best that I leave. And without a word, I turned around and walked out. By the time I got to my car, I was shaking like a leave. Betrayed. The ultimate betrayal. My throat hurt. I could not swallow down the pain that has made its residence in my throat. I could not nurse the grief that I felt, could not patch my soul or heart together. How I got home is a miracle, as I have absolutely no recollection of getting or driving there. I simply went to my room, got in bed, and cried myself to sleep. Heaving from the heartache, choking on the hurt in my throat, I spent a restless night, waking often, crying the whole time. And came to a startling revelation: Zoe has been my soulmate, but I have never been hers. And despite what the future brings us, I would never be her soulmate. Few people in life are fortunate enough to meet theirs. Even fewer are fortunate to have it reciprocated. I found mine, but Zoe was still searching for hers, potentially settled for second best knowing that the quest may lead to never finding the one true soul that she has been longing for.

The next day at work, Zoe called me and asked if I would come over that evening. It was Thursday and would have been our regular evening together, but after what happened, I wasn't sure if I would go and was also not sure if she wanted me to come over. But she did. I felt nothing at all for being asked to come over. I knew we had to discuss what had happened, and then find a way forward, whether together or separated. But I needed to understand how I missed the signs and what caused the love of my life, the one true soulmate of mine to destroy what we had in a fleeting moment of lust and debauchery. To be in a more than three year relationship and have carnal affairs with someone other than your lover speaks volumes of the person. Clearly, I did not know Zoe as well as I thought I did. And in one moment of adultery, she broke the perfect trust that existed between us and scattered it like shards of glass.

That evening I ate at home first and then went over to Zoe's. She had cooked for both of us but I told her that I have already eaten. I had nothing further to say, so I waited for her explanation.

"I don't know where to begin," Zoe started.

I immediately interrupted her. "Don't start off by telling me you are sorry. I don't want to hear it. You are not sorry. For if you were sorry, then you would never have done this in the first place. So don't you dare tell me you are sorry."

"Ok," Zoe said, "I won't. It doesn't mean that I am not, but I won't say it."

I simply looked at her and waited for an explanation.

"For a while now I have been unhappy in our relationship," Zoe started to explain. "Our life has become mundane. Routine. We do the same things, have the same discussions, and somehow some of the excitement has left our relationship. On top of that, your overbearing personality has made me feel smothered. You always knowing best. You tell me how to do things, where to go, what to do, when to do it. To the extent that I started feeling as if I could not think for myself, as if I was unable to think for myself. That you had to guide me, be there for me, and be the strong one. And by you being strong, telling me what to do, you made me feel weak. You made me feel insecure. You always want to have the final say; your decisions are the ones that stand. You never change your mind, but expect me to change mine. And so I wanted to feel strong again. Strong. Not cocooned, not protected. Strong. Someone who doesn't believe that they need to guide me. I didn't want someone telling me what to do, how to do it or when to do it. And so by chance, I ran into Michael again. And he was everything that you are not. He allowed me to take charge, to make decisions, to do what I wanted, how I wanted, when I wanted. And one thing led to another, and in my moment of utter despair and weakness, we had sex. It meant nothing to me other than physically bonding with one person who I felt doesn't and couldn't control me. I don't want to be controlled. I am not yours to control. I want to feel as if I am your equal, never your inferior. Michael was a pawn, but also a mistake. It will never happen again. But I cannot go on if things are not going to change. I have taken leave from work and will be going away. I need to clear my mind, I need a new perspective, and going away is the only way that I can see will get me through this. As I need to feel strong again, and not weak. And around you, I feel weak."

So in the end, I was the one who drove Zoe into another man's arms. This is what she was saying. By the very core of who I was, my personality, my actions, my reactions, my very being, all of it caused her to seek another. How does one ever move forward, when the actual root of the problem is me? I cannot change my core being, I am who I am. Sure, I can try to be on the lookout when I am perceived to be dominating, or when I am prescriptive, but what will happen if I falter, if I fall, if I fail, as I am fallible. Will this lead to another transgression?

"What do you want me to say, Zoe?" I asked. "Clearly, the person who I am is not the right one for you."

"Don't say that! Give me time. Time will get me through this. But I need time, and you need to be patient if our survival means anything to you."

Cold, calculated and somehow dominating, this is what Zoe was expecting from me.

I agreed to give Zoe all the time in the world, thinking to myself that while she was working out how to be stronger, I had to cope with how to trust her again, how to overcome the destruction of betrayal, of infidelity. How to look at her, knowing that another touched her in only a way I should. That I was hurt was not foremost in her mind, that I was betrayed was not a thought she dwelled on. But more so, that she judged and criticised my very being, of who I was. And that she never in three years' time let on that this was a problem. That the first time I had to find out about it was not in a conversation between two lovers talking about building and making stronger

134

their relationship. No, I had to find out by finding her in another man's arms. And wondered whether she would have ever told me had I not walked in on her moment of shameful and reckless abandonment.

Over the next couple of weeks, Zoe spent time on her own, and after returning to work again she continued to ask for alone time, as she slowly believed that she was starting to make progress. Zoe insisted that we continued seeing each other at least once a week, as she had to learn to cope to accept me and my strong, and according to her, sometimes overwhelming personality. She insisted that I also sleep over on alternate weekends, as this would ensure that she is aware of me being in her life the whole time and that she had to accept the very person that I was. However, I was not to be amorous and making love was totally out of the question. I also during this period could not share a bed with her, so although I was sleeping over, I was made to sleep in the spare bedroom. So Zoe started to cope with her feelings, and during this whole ordeal, she never once considered what her time out was doing to me. She continued as if we were in a loving relationship, sans the loving part, not once broaching the topic of actually discussing this with me. She at times requested that I take her shopping or to a manicure and wait for an hour in the car until she finished, to then take her back to her place.

"Zoe, is there perhaps an opportunity for us to seek counselling together?" I enquired one evening.

"For what?"

"Well, I don't see how you can make progress if you don't even get to understand who I am. I am the core of your problem, yet you never once asked me to discuss my feelings with me on everything that you blamed me for."

"This is not about you. This is about me. So don't go and psychoanalyse this. Let it be and give me the time I asked."

Although I felt like exploding on the one side and still hurting on the other side, I knew that if I had to have a full-out blow-up, that this would only alienate Zoe even further. I had to accept that I was the reason why she had to go through this ordeal, that I was the cause of her problems, and that by her trying to work through it, it meant she loved me and wanted to find a way to stay with me and accept me for who I am.

In the third month of her self-searching mission, I one evening in a moment of despair, loneliness, isolation and deprivation, tried to get Zoe to touch me. I took her in my arms and started kissing her neck, her earlobes, and guiding her hands slowly down to my eagerness. But Zoe withdrew and accused me of confusing her, that she needed the space and that I should not overstep the boundaries that were set between us.

"What boundaries?" I yelled at Zoe. "How can you work on loving me as a person when you cringe at the very thought of me touching you?" I blurted out.

"I must first love the person again, you again before I make love to you again. Can't you understand that?"

"The person. Dear Lord! We are talking about me. Call me by my damn name! And what do you mean love me again? Have you stopped loving me and now you are trying to convince yourself to love me again?"

"It is complicated. I asked for time and you agreed. This does not look like agreeing to me any longer."

"You know what, Zoe. I think it best if I leave. For I will surely say something that I will regret and that I can never take back."

And without a further word, I left Zoe's townhouse and went home. Three months of not dealing with my hurt and sadness all came to a boiling rage, and I needed to get out of there as quickly as I could. Three months of not being able to talk about my feelings, my pain, my loss and my sadness. That I only had to focus on Zoe, her needs, her desires and had to play it by her rules. That I had to be careful of who I was, as it was me, my soul, my very being that caused her to drift away and right into the arms of a willing suitor.

Three months after I walked out that evening, Zoe called me at work and asked me to come over.

"I am ready to move on to the next phase, the phase of allowing you fully into my life again," Zoe said as I entered the front door, only too eager to let me know what her decision was.

But for me, this was too late. Her self-centredness, even egotistical approach to resolving our issues left me in the dark. Although I still loved her with everything that I had in me, that she would always be my soulmate, I realised that I could never trust Zoe again. That it took me three months of hell living with my soulmate who treated me like a stranger, not a lover. That she only thought of her recovery, her reason for straying, never once giving me a thought. Perhaps then I saw her for who she truly was for the first time in my life. That it always was only around her and her needs, and with me having a voice, a strong personality and wanting an equal opportunity in our relationship, she set her sights on a weaker prey. That had I not caught her in bed with another man, she would have eventually floundered in our relationship and would have walked away. All that took place was that the inevitable was postponed. One day in the future, I am perhaps going to say the wrong thing, perhaps telling her what to do, not because I am controlling but simply because I cared. And this would cause her to once again cheat on me. Knowing all of this, realising it all, sadly at the most inopportune time when Zoe was ready to move forward again, I came to the conclusion that I had to end our relationship.

"Zoe," I started. "It has been three long months, where while you were sorting out your feelings, I was alone coping with my hurt, my feelings, my pain. During all this time, you never once asked me about how I was feeling, from the start you blamed me and because you blamed me, somehow, it seemed righteous to you that you could screw around and hurt me. I am glad that you have learnt how to deal with a strong personality, how to deal with a strong person, but I know now, I could never go on like this."

"What do you mean?" Zoe interrupted.

"Please let me finish. I will always wonder what you are up to when I am not with you. If you are late, I will always be suspicious and think the worse. I will never be able to trust you, and once trust is broken, it can never be mended, not even repaired. You brought an injustice upon us. You destroyed something so sacred and of such value to me without hesitation. Your coldness in dealing with your problem pushed me away instead of embracing me. And I have come to terms that although I will always love you, with all my heart, that I will never be able to be with you. That I was one of the few people in the world who can honestly state that I have met my soulmate. Sadly, you cannot say the same. And that is all right with me. I was always happy with it being a fifty per cent treasure, but no longer. It is over. I will not ask you to be friends, as I could never bear the thought of being your friend and seeing you with someone else. The last three years of my life was the best time I ever had, you showed me how to love and be loved. But you tore me apart. Some parts will never be found again, they have withered away, scorched and singed."

"Please, don't say that. Don't be rash. I now know where it all went wrong and how to deal with it. Please, let's give it one more try. You owe me that much."

"Zoe, Zoe, Zoe. Again, your plea is all about you, your needs. Not once have you asked for forgiveness, not once have you said you were sorry for what you have done to me. Enough about you. Now it is about me. So, no, Zoe, although you will never know how much it pains me to say these words, there is no moving forward for us. It is over. Done with. I don't ever want to see you in my life again."

And with those words, I got in my car and drove away, never once looking back and never once making contact with Zoe again. To this day, I have no idea what happened to her, and I have never once run into her. It has now been more than a decade that this happened, and I have never been in a serious relationship ever again. And never will get into another relationship, as I firmly believe that in this life, one only has one soulmate and I met and subsequently lost mine. Hopefully, by now, Zoe has met hers.

***

By ending the call today, I closed this chapter once and for all. Being betrayed, being accused of the reason why the betrayal all took place in the first place, after all these years, I realised the hurt has never dissipated. That I lost my soulmate but was lucky enough at least to be able to find her in the first place. But that there truly is only ever one soulmate for each of us, and therefore, I will never love again, as I simply would not be able to love the person as much as I loved Zoe. And that realisation made the pain and the hurt a little bit more bearable.

Thinking that maybe I was too hasty not to take the call, hoping for and against a call back, I knew that I now had the number and that at any time, I could call it. It slowly dawned on me that this would be disastrous for both of us. So I took my iPhone, opened the contacts and blocked the caller, both in terms of receiving calls and messages on all platforms available. I simply did not want Zoe back in my life again, not after all this time.

Feeling colder than I was a few minutes ago, looking at my watch I realised it was past lunchtime already. Where has the time gone to? What has happened to this day? This most certainly was not the easiest stroll down memory lane, but somehow I felt that it was needed, that I needed to clear my thoughts. As the dream and the song and now the call finally had all caused what was bubbling inside of me to boil over. And that I had to face the onslaughts of the soul destroyers to in the end be able to defend and heal my soul. And to be healed became an insatiable hunger.

But I realised that I needed some time away from it all, from the memories and that I needed a distraction. I took my cell phone and called Sis.

"Hey Sis, what are you up to?" I asked.

"Nothing much," Sis replied. "This is your kind of weather. But I find it so depressing. And I am cold so I thought today I am not sticking my nose outside of this house."

"Yeah, it is cold. But I haven't had lunch yet and thought maybe you would like to join me for a late lunch?"

"Where do you want to go?" Sis enquired.

"What about the usual place. You know I just love their food."

"Ok, let me take a shower first and then I will meet you there."

"See you in 30 minutes."

So I dressed to go out in the weather, looked for a beanie to cover my head, went down the stairs and got in my car and drove to our usual place for lunch. The rain was incessant, and with the grey and thick clouds and the plummeting temperature, my torrential feelings at times threatened to overwhelm me, causing me to drive faster than I should in the bad weather, with slippery roads and careless drivers on the road, making for very dangerous conditions.

Slow down, I told myself, knowing very well that I was too eager for companionship on this cold day, to escape if only for a few hours the memories that threatened to haunt me the entire day. Arriving, I noticed that Sis was not there yet. I entered the restaurant, and as I was a familiar face there, there was no need for me to place my order for drinks, as it was well known.

A few minutes later Sis walked in, not happy to be out in the cold. But the restaurant was warm and this thawed her mood somewhat.

"What have you been up to today?" Sis asked.

I told Sis about waking up from a bad dream, not giving too many details of the dream, and then with the song on the radio, I told her the floodgates of my memory banks were broken and that I spent the entire morning reliving many of my past experiences.

"It is normal for this to happen. Accept it and go with its stride." Sis recommended.

"How can it be normal?" I asked Sis.

"Really? Are you going to deny yourself the fact? Are you going to suppress the memory and pretend that there is really no reason for the mood you are in?"

With a start, I realised what Sis was referring to. How is it possible that I have completely forgotten about it? That I have willingly forced myself to not stare the hard cold facts in the face.

Fortunately, I was saved by the manageress who confirmed Sis' order, as my order always is the same. Sis ordered her food, and we sat back and just enjoyed spending time together.

In order not to face the reality of my cause for not con-fronting the day, I changed the topic and Sis and I started talking about her work, about the challenges she faced and about the fact that she enjoyed the contribution she made. That she had a passion for her job, for the people she worked with and that she was glad that she was making a difference and changing the area.

Our food arrived and as always, the quality of the food was superb. We relished and devoured the food, which filled us with warmth against the onslaughts of this very cold and wet winter's day. And as always, Sis and I were very comfortable in each other's presence, as there was no need for constant conversation, as even certain silences between siblings were relaxed and created contentment between us.

After enjoying our food, we both returned home, Sis had some work that she needed to do, and I needed to confront the reasons for my dark mood, which were aided and abet-ted by the dream and the song on the radio. Driving home, I replayed some of the conversation around Sis and her career, and involuntarily, I was thinking of my career, and how even in my career I was betrayed. Different betrayal, but damaging nonetheless.

WORK POLITICS

My career has always been important to me, and from an early age on I had a drive and decided that success only comes with the status that you achieve at work and that this was what I was working towards. Today, when I look back over more than two decades of being in a professional career, I am joyous of the fact that I was quite successful and that I reached the level in the organisation that I always aspired to. But reaching that level has not come without challenges, many that could be dealt with in an easy way, others in a more difficult way, and others yet never able to be dealt with.

About seven years ago, I was promoted to a senior level within the organisation that I was working for, and at the time had just over sixty per cent of the staff complement of the business unit reporting into my area of control and responsibility. With having a strong personality and always believing that one calls a spade a spade, not a shovel, not a digging tool, I was known to be quite blunt at times with staff reporting into my area of responsibility. Over time, one learns how to address staff, when and where it was best to have serious discussions and overall ensuring that albeit that one's point of view is brought across in a serious and disciplined way that the staff members always knew and understood that this was done with respect. Hence, I firmly believe even today that my staff understood me, knew that I respected them, comprehended that the serious discussions related to the issue and never the person, and in general, I felt I had a good rapport and relationship with my team.

During this time, the relationship I had with my immediate superior soured for many different reasons. It started with my superior not recognising my team's or my own achievements.

"Why is it that the operational team is always excluded when it comes to recognising success?" I asked of my superior.

"Operations as a function is very hard to evaluate, as staff needs to do what they are contracted to do."

"I agree. But where staff walk the extra mile and do so much more, that they constantly raise the bar and epitomise what quality customer service is all about, then surely this should be recognised, especially when this is highlighted, as is so often the case."

But due to my audacity to disagree, this created a wedge in the working relationship that I had with my boss. However, with my direct approach with and to managing staff, and it not always being liked due to people being different and having different personalities, my boss decided that it was time to show that staff did not like a direct approach.

"I need our staff members to be allowed to have a bigger voice, and so I have decided to have an intervention with the teams, but with one caveat, none of the managerial team members will be present during these open discussions with the team," my boss announced to the management team.

Albeit that there was an ulterior motive behind this move, I and the rest of the senior management team also felt that it was a great means to get staff members to open up on how to create a better working environment for all, so that we understood where we were in terms of overall staff satisfaction. I also believed that the results would speak for themselves and that my boss would be surprised by the results and not necessarily achieve what was in my opinion underhandedly decided upon.

So our Human Resources Department was called in to conduct different informal sessions with the team, and they broke these sessions down in different categories, ranging from what made staff wanted to give a thumbs up, and what caused staff to want to give a thumbs down. From these, action plans then had to be set up so that we as a business unit could improve on the thumbs down issues and we continued to excel on the thumbs up accolades.

Staff members were both excited and cautious and some even downright dubious with regards to the reason for the sessions. As a management team, we encouraged staff members to attend, to open up and to make our business unit a great place to work for.

Once the sessions with the staff members were concluded, from these discussions, we received a report per area and business unit, and my business unit was no exception. We had by far more thumbs down entries than we had thumbs up entries. The task was to now address these issues with the staff concerned and see where we could improve.

Not all the comments or the thumbs down entries were directed at me as the head of the area, but there were a few that clearly indicated some room for improvement on my side. At times, certain comments were quite personal, that I felt that the very core of who I was, my entire being, was being attacked, criticised and judged. Although I felt that staff understood where I was coming from, I wasn't entirely prepared for this reality. But for me, this was an opportunity to make some wrongs right, as even though I felt that there certainly was no basis to become personal, that I would take constructively from the criticism received and turn it around in favour of all. And I could see that the reports exceeded my boss's expectation in that there were more positives than negatives in terms of the outcomes.

Naturally, after each of the sessions, despite the fact that staff members were requested to not discuss what transpired during these sessions and rather to wait for the outcomes as disclosed in the reports, some staff members ignored this and spoke openly of their dismay during these sessions. A few people that I worked with, to my surprise, I learned did not contribute to any of the discussions that took place. Not in a negative way or in a positive way. They absorbed what was said, but whether they agreed or disagreed, they never once felt it was necessary to voice their opinions.

Action plans were put in place, the report was discussed with the management team, and I also addressed the report in each of the team meetings that I attended. I made it clear to staff members that we appreciated their input and that we all had to work towards one common goal. Fixing the things that needed fixing and to continue to do well where we excelled.

A while later, a follow-up exercise was done with the teams again to gauge the morale of staff, and staff members were asked to again raise any concerns, any comments that they may have and place these in a confidential box, as to see whether there was any improvement on the previous exercise. And indeed, there was a great improvement, as there were now even fewer concerns than previously, but there indeed were still issues that needed attendance. And although I viewed these exercises as imperative to build staff morale, I also was of the opinion that staff members would hide behind the anonymity. Despite asking staff that when they assess an area or a person, that they needed to look at indicative behaviour and not a once off disagreement, I still felt that this was a playing field for staff to get back at management. Surprisingly, there were a few compliments also raised by staff members, which meant we were getting closer to a balanced view, but that there was still a lot of hard work involved.

As the notes were anonymous, we never knew who contributed the comments, and this was of no importance at all. However, in discussions that I had with the teams and with staff in general before the exercise took place, some of them were quite open and I believed honest with me and shared with me the areas my team, my unit or I was strong in and the areas that needed to be improved upon. So naturally, I expected the areas that were highlighted as strong would also become apparent in the exercise undertaken by the staff members concerned.

However, again to my surprise, once we analysed the comments and the overall constructive criticism received, I recognised some of the areas where we improved upon based on the comments received during discussions with the teams, the teams and individuals elected not to mention during the exercise. They neglected to record the compliments they bestowed on my team or my area, which made me ponder whether the compliments were real, or were they merely mentioned in passing to sound as if they had a balanced view.

I never expected this; I always only ever wanted the truth. If this was what they could share with me, then the question I had in my mind was why it was not important enough for them to share it as part of their comments when they were in the group discussions or when they had the opportunity to place their comments in the confidential box. I felt completely betrayed by the very people that I thought I could rely on, that were colleagues but that I also considered as friends. In the end, when they had the opportunity to rescue my team and my area from the burning stake, they were the first to set it alight by their silence.

And an old realisation dawned upon me in that people will always disappoint you, that no matter what they say, they are always in it first for themselves, and very seldom for anyone else. Granted, when the overall results were discussed with the group of staff, many of them pointed out that they completely forgot to mention the good, that they felt only obligated to mention the areas that could be improved on. They rationalised that overall by having fewer areas in need of improvement, the overall results would have been more positive, so by not saying it outright to them would not have made a difference when the results were tallied. I had a completely different view to this, as I firmly believed that even the areas of success had to be pointed out and be shared and in fact celebrated as achievements and improvements. So I remained betrayed by a special group of colleagues and friends, despite the fact that we had different viewpoints on the overall approach. As this was my perception, it became my reality, and once again, in life, I learned that I had to fend for myself and not rely on anyone. And as I shared my feeling of betrayal with the team members, I believe that many of them would approach the issue differently the next time they had the opportunity to voice their opinions.

***

I stopped at home, parked the car and walked up the stairs. I took off my beanie, set the air conditioner on heat, took a blanket and went to lie down in the bay window again. And thinking that even though I felt betrayed by my colleagues and friends, that in the end, their loyalty to me stood the test of time. That where it was needed later, they defended my area, my teams, or me and that I had to see the bigger picture, and experience it from their point of view. And albeit that they knew I was disappointed in them, as I voiced it in my discussions, they also knew that I did not dwell on it. But lying in the bay window, with the raindrops pelting the window, creating a steady beat, I knew that although my soul felt betrayed, that these friends stood by me for many years, that we all are fallible, that I even may have failed them somewhere along the road, and they accepted it as they accepted me. And the hole created by this betrayal started to be filled with the love of acceptance and friend-ship. And that even though the hole itself will never recover completely, knowing what I know now, having the benefit of hindsight, it made the experience less hurtful.

And just like that, thinking of hurt and soul-ache, my mind again took off, and I remembered. Other causes and other holes. This indeed was a day where my mood simply matched the weather.

4

THE HOLE OF HUMILIATION

My father's biggest aspiration was to teach me the art of boxing; however, I abhorred the violence I associated with the sport. Perhaps again, being so protected by the female species of our household, by Mom and Sis, who absolutely understood and witnessed my father's deep hatred of and for me, their fussing over me made me in hindsight perhaps a tad softer than what a boy of my age should be.

Nevertheless, my father believed he had an answer for this, and at the times when I simply could not escape my father, he would line up some suitable contenders that I needed to box against and he would pay them a handsome reward (as considered handsome by a child) if they beat me. If they lost, they would still receive a few cents but if they won the reward would be quite more substantial.

In the late 1970s, to get fifty or sixty cents was a lot of money for the youngsters and therefore, there never was a shortage of prize fighting contenders that I had to face. Win or lose, I never got a single bob from my father, but I had to ensure that I faced each challenge with vigour.

"Come ye, come forward lads," my father would call to a group of boys on their way home from school.

"Yes, sir?" the leader of the group would usually pipe up, as in those days, respecting older people was one of the key values ingrained with children, and speaking to strangers were not frowned upon as it is in these days.

"Fancy making some money, do you?" my father would continue, setting me up as always.

"Yes, sir!" The boys would chorus in unison.

Living in Tranquillity one had to take whatever one could and if a stranger offered you money for some hard toil, well then you go about and do what is needed from you. In any case, by now, my father was renowned with most of the boys in Tranquillity and they knew what he was up to.

"Well, then," he said. "Anyone who could beat this sorry excuse's ass will get five bob from me. So who is game?"

Fifty cents. Fifty cents to the boys were prize money of note. Fifty cents to humiliate me, to beat me and even to degrade me even more in the eyes of my father. Somehow, he always managed to have some spare change around on those days where I particularly was a bane in his life.

"I will, sir," the strongest, tallest and leader of the group proclaimed.

My father would then take two sets of boxing gloves then made a makeshift boxing ring, glove us up, pretending to be the referee and give us the rules.

"Best out of three rounds, winner takes all. Loser gets nothing. No punches to the face, if you do, you are disqualified. Only blows to the body, and if you are able to hit the jaw, use an uppercut. But be warned, boys. If I see as much as a blow to the face above the jawline, you will be thrown out of the ring and you will forfeit your prize money," he would declare.

I mostly tried to avoid my father, but on days when Mom was busy making a living or was not at home, and Sis was also no-where near and I was unfortunate enough to be with him, these days proved to be taxing and trying. And on these days, I had no choice but to enter the makeshift ring and boxed.

So we squared up, my father told us to go to our corners and then sounded the bell. He used an empty wine bottle and a spoon, and the "clank" sound was the start of round number one. Out came the leader of the group, fierce and ready for a battle, knowing very well that he would whip me with ease. He came at me with punches and blows from left and right and all I could do was retreat, trying to block, to avert to dodge and to stay on my feet. Thirty seconds into round one, he walloped me and I was knocked down. Staying down was not an option because the spitting and fiery tirade that I would have to endure from my father's tongue was more damaging than getting a beating with boxing gloves. So I stood up, tried to land a few weak blows, some of them not so weak, and before I knew it, the end of round one was donged by the bottle and spoon bell. My father then would also declare at the end of each round the winner, and due to me being floored, my father declared my opponent as the winner of round one.

Heaving, breathing hard, trying to take the sting of humiliation and of being hurt out of my eyes, I heard the distant dong announcing that round number two has started. I needed to work out a strategy and fast as well. For if I went in there and was floored again, I would lose the boxing match, which was a given in any event, but I knew how much worse it was going to be if I don't at least try and take one round off my opponent.

So in I went, low, dodging the blows to my body, and then I saw an opening, and I let go with one triumphant blow to his midsection. Whilst hitting him in his tummy, I could hear and feel the sudden whoosh of his wind leaving him, and followed that up with a punch to the jaw. Down he went and he crawled with pain. I retired to my corner, bouncing around, elated that I had the fortune and luck of the blows that floored my opponent. Sadly, this elation was cut short as my opponent stood up, and more determined than ever he came in with a ferocity of a wounded animal. And within seconds he gave me a beating and I fell down, waiting for the round to be over. And the bell was rung, and my father declared the boy the winner. And promptly paid him his fifty cents. Laughing joyously, the boys went off to go and spend their money in a befitting way.

My father then made me clean up the makeshift area, more so that Mom and Sis do not witness the aftermath of his actions. And during this, he would scornfully remind me how he rued the day that I was born. That I was too weak to carry the family genes forward. That I would never aspire to anything, that I would be a failure. That he was too ashamed to call me his son, and that he is even more regretful that I shared his name. I simply kept quiet, my head bowed down low so that my father could not see the tears I cried. Humiliated, hated, blamed and so utterly disliked for who I was. And there was nothing, simply not a thing that I could do to change the way he felt about me.

There were times that I was fortunate and that I was able to beat an opponent. On those occasions, my father would pay less than offered to the boy, walked away in disgust. I never was sure if he was disgusted because of me being able to beat an opponent, or if he was disgusted with my opponent being beaten.

One particular day, my father had another fight lined up and in mind for me, where the contender was someone that I had boxed and beaten before. However, hoping for money, this poor soul would consistently come back for a hiding, and despite the fact that I beat the living daylights out of this boy, my father was never satisfied with my achievement.

After this particular boxing match where I again was the victor, my father walked away, shaking his head and muttering insults under his breath, most of them referring to me as a sissy boy or nancy boy, and at times, when he was particularly nasty, he would refer to me as a faggot. "Stupid faggot. Fighting with his hands all dandy and in the air," he would mutter under his breath. "No child of mine can be this queer."

Despite not understanding what it really meant, those words cut deeply, every time, like a serrated knife, sawing its way through my soul, leaving a raw piece of meat dangling deep inside of me. I did not know what a faggot was. My understanding of a sissy boy was a boy softer than others, perhaps a little more fragile, but is that so wrong?

As a result of constantly being called a faggot, and no longer wanting to become my father's source of pleasure when I was boxing and beaten, I withdrew and grew more into my shell, avoiding my father at all costs and spending more and more time with Sis and Mom. And obviously, any boy in his life needed a role model to base his experiences on, to learn from and to be taught what is expected of being a boy. This was sadly lacking as Mom and Sis tried very hard, but unfortunately, the only thing that I did was either playing with Sis and her friends, or being with Mom, visiting her friends in Tranquillity.

"Mom," I asked one day whilst walking home with Mom after visiting one of her friends. "What is a faggot?"

"Where did you hear this word?" Mom was flustered.

"I overheard a few boys talking, Mom," I evaded telling Mom the full truth.

"It is the most derogatory word ever. People use this word to hurt others. It is hurtful and it is cruel," Mom said.

"Yes, Mom. But what does it mean?"

"You are too young to understand the meaning of the word. Just know this. No one has the right to call anyone by this name. No one. And promise me that you will never ever use this word, you will not taunt or tease anyone and you would not call anyone by this name?"

Me? I thought. Calling anyone by that name. How could I, when I did not understand what it meant? That I was the very source of ridicule. That I was called that name. It had to be something terrible if Mom did not even say the word and made me promise never to use it.

"I promise." I solemnly declared to Mom, not really understanding why but knowing deep down that it was the right thing to do.

And for some unknown reason, even other boys of my age and older also considered me to be a faggot as well, for surely if my father could call me a faggot in front of them as often as he did, surely they would recognise that I was different. Despite my trying to box them and sometimes winning but mostly losing, perhaps just to piss my father off more, this did nothing for my reputation amongst boys. And when they would walk by and they would see me, they would laugh and point at me, sneer and call me names. And all I could do was take it, let it wash over me like a crashing wave, sweeping me emotionally off my feet. Not knowing how to react or what to do differently to escape this torture.

A few boys at primary school took pity on me and were happy to be my friends, but at times I could also see the accusatory and disapproving look in their eyes when I did something particularly un-boy-like. Therefore, due to these friends, hardly coming over to play after school, tea parties and dressing up games became the order of the day with Sis, and all of this only fuelled my father's hatred and loathing of and for me. As I grew older, I first started resenting my father, then starting hating my father, and finally grew apathetic towards anything that would and could befall my father.

My father, I am told always had a good singing voice, and my mother and father both loved to dance. Perhaps this is where I inherited my love for music. At the age of six, at one of those very seldom occasions where there were funds available towards a proper Christmas present, as Mom again saved money during the course of the year from her gambling commission earned, Mom asked us to write a letter to Santa and ask him for a gift.

"Only ask Santa for one gift," Mom admonished us. "We don't want Santa to think we are a greedy family in Tranquillity."

One gift. I immediately knew what I wanted. I eagerly wanted it for such a long time and now maybe, just maybe Santa would be smiling upon our family and give me the best present ever.

"Dear Santa," I wrote. "It must be nice for you to be in warm weather now, as Mom told me that you are coming to our town. I hope you are not going to sweat too much in your suit, but we have some water in the tap if you visit and if you are thirsty.

"Santa, please would you be so kind and bring me a record player turntable, you know, the ones that play the 45 singles or long play records. Please Santa. As you did not visit us last year and I think I was good, please Santa. Thank you, Santa. Don't forget to drink some water if you are hot."

On Christmas day, I woke up and looked under my bed, as we had no Christmas tree. Wow! Santa was here. Santa Clause came to town, and he showered me with a turntable with a built-in speaker. I loved it, and could now play music to my heart's content.

My father, on the other hand, viewed this as an atrocity adding to my already queer and faggot ways. After several times warning me to switch off the damn thing, he finally stomped over to where I was blissfully ignorant and ignoring him, kicked my Santa Clause gift against the wall and brought my Christmas present to a crashing end. I howled as if it was the end of the world, Mom was all over my father, gnashing and gnawing but in the end, nothing could resurrect my record player again. Money was saved over a long period to buy this special gift for me and none was available to replenish the loss.

Being close to Mom and Sis, and being called a faggot and queer, life indeed became very difficult. So difficult that I continued to withdraw into my own shell and started escaping by reading books. As I didn't have many friends as most of the boys that I knew echoed my father's sentiments and called me a faggot as well. The only two close friends though that accepted me for whom and what I was in primary school became my best friends I could ever have at the time, and we became inseparable at school and even at times after school.

One day we decided that we needed to have a home base where we could convene and make plans of what we were going to do and what games we were going to play. To do this, we could not do it at any of our homes, as parents often would interrupt and walk in on us in our rooms, and we needed time away from adults. A place of our own. So we decided that the best thing to do was to build ourselves a tree house. Once we decided where we were going to build the tree house, we started on this task immediately. Although I knew nothing of tools and building tree houses or even carpentry for that matter, I was part of this team and would help carry and do what I was told to do. We were kept busy until late at night during this particular primary school holiday. While we were busy, some other rather nasty boy who was probably five or six years older than we were climbed in the tree and blocked us from getting out. When he saw me he used the same words that my father called me trying to intimidate me.

"Oh, looky at what we have here. If it isn't the little faggot and *her* friends."

"Leave us be," my one friend, challenged the bully.

"You shut up, or else I will hit the living shit out of you." The bully promised him a hiding.

"So, the faggot and *her* friends are up here in a tree. Tell me faggot, where did you learn to use the tools to make a tree house?"

I did not say a word. I was hurt, again, at hearing this one word used to describe who I was, one word that tore me to pieces and broke me apart. But I was not about to let this fool see it. So for my silence, he took a torch and he shone it in my eyes. I refused to blink. You can call me all the names you like but I will never succumb, was what I was thinking the whole time he had that damn light in my eyes. He was quite taken aback at my audacity, as he did not expect this reaction from me. Although I could box, physical violence was against everything that I believed in and hence I refused to fight. I also knew that there was no way that I could ever beat this boy, that he would not relent until the blood flowed. Indeed, there was an element as well of being afraid of getting hurt. And this boy was so much older than we were. And he disliked me so intensely, perhaps even hated me. More so when he believed what I would become one day.

"Why do you two even bother to spend time with this faggot?" he asked my friends.

They wisely chose not the answer him, sensing that whatever answer they gave would enrage him. He had plans for us, but could not execute it in the tree. So by still shining the light in our eyes, he ordered us one by one to get out of the tree and wait until everybody has assembled. He told my friends that if any one of them ran, the last one in the tree will not only get a beating but will be thrown from the tree as well. So my friends were concerned and therefore waited as was instructed by this bully. I was the last to get out of the tree, and I knew that I had to do something, else we were in for a hiding and a beating. Mustering all the courage and resolve I had, as I started to climb down the tree, I saw an opening and pushed him aside. He had to grab hold of a branch to not lose his footing and fall from the tree and this was all that we needed to make a run for it and escaped this boy.

"I will get you! You faggot! You and your two friends. I will wait for you in your tree house and I will beat the shit out of you. I will get you!" he shouted.

While walking home later that evening, knowing that our tree house was something of the past and very short lived, with tears running from my eyes and streaming down my face, I hated it what I was called. I hated the word. I hated what it was supposed to have meant. And I thought to myself: my father must be right, for if others who were not family who do not know me believe that I am a faggot then surely I must be one. The pain and the hurt of what that one word can do cannot be described. So I cowered away from anyone who would or could ever inflict such emotional pain on me. How do you look friends in the eye when others are calling you by this name? This hole in my soul was going to be around for a long time. And although I did not understand what the word meant, I instinctively knew it had to do with boys not behaving like boys. How boys were supposed to behave I was not too sure of, I did box, although, against my will, I did play with other boys my age, we fooled around and played all the boy games, but somehow, this was not enough. I had been labelled, and this would be my cross to bear.

AND THEN THERE WERE TWO

s a young boy, being estranged from other boys except for my two close friends who accepted me for me, due to these other boys considering me as different and some even thinking and calling me a faggot, I was a loner and kept to myself most of the times. Other than these two very good primary school friends that I had, there were times that we could not be together as they would go away on holidays or to family members, and at these times I would rather keep to myself than seeking the presence of other playmates. This was also the case at one time in primary school when both my mates were booked off ill when an infection of pink eye was doing the rounds at our school. I was fortunate enough to escape the clutches of this infection, but many of the schoolchildren were booked off and kept at home to prevent a further spread of the disease.

During this time, with so many children being booked off school, normal classes could not resume as this would have affected too many children. As a result, the school decided that they would over the fortnight that the children were booked off, have more physical training events during school hours. This was to ensure that they made good with the time they had on the one hand, and with the added benefit that some of the more sporty and active scholars would get more time to exercise and practice their routine. This, however, meant that all scholars were required to partake in a sports activity. At the time, I chose the long distance event as I felt I had the necessary built and stamina to do ten rounds around the rugby field. This was exhausting but I enjoyed it at the time, although not particularly good at it. But it kept us busy, and we worked up a sweat. After training, we were required to hit the showers, and then attend some other non-curriculum classes until school was out.

I never had a problem hitting the showers with other boys, and never wondered about things like genitals. However, on this one occasion, one particular boy who played rugby and was a few grades ahead of us also hit the showers, and he made fun of everyone in the showers. This was taken in good spirit. This boy, however, stopped at my shower stall, and as I exited he started to laugh. He rolled on the ground and pointed to me and at the top of his lungs he roared and shouted, "One ball, one ball, the faggot only has one ball!"

I was mortified. What does he mean I only have one testicle? How many are you supposed to have? When everyone laughed and some showed me that they had two, I covered my crotch with a towel, too ashamed and humiliated to let them continue seeing my malformed genitals. I got dressed as quickly as I could, and as this was the last thing we had to do before school was out, I raced home sobbing.

"Mom, Mom!" I shouted, swiftly bypassing my father who was sitting on the porch, starting to exchange sobriety for inebriation. I did not even think of talking to my father about this fact.

"What is it, my dear child? Why are you crying like this?"

"Mom, why did you not tell me that I am malformed, that I should have two balls instead of only one?"

"My dear child," Mom started grabbing me and hugging me fiercely.

"First of all, we do not call them 'balls'. If you have to refer to them, you call them testicles. Nevertheless, don't fret about it, child. We spoke to the doctor a long time ago and he said that the one will drop when you are older."

"Drop from where?" I asked, stupefied.

Mom could not help but smile. "Why, my son, you also have two, always had two. Yours is just high up in your belly and one day will drop down into its own sac, into its proper place."

Although I was relieved to have learnt that one day I will not be different in physical appearances to other boys, the damage unfortunately was done. I never afterwards could go into a shower and be comfortable standing naked in front of other boys. And as a result of this humiliation, I also had problems standing at a urinal and pass water, in the event that another boy may come in and see my difference. And this became a mental obstacle for me to be part of me for the rest of my life, even today, despite the fact that in Standard 9 (Grade 11), out of the blue, one day I noticed that there were two. The humiliation of being laughed at, coupled with the fact that I was considered different and a faggot, took its toll on my psyche and by implication, on my soul.

A RUGBY COACH'S HATRED

One day, Peter with the coppery red hair and freckles and Rudy, the shy blonde boy with the reflection of the sky in his eyes, my two best friends in primary school mentioned to me that they were going to try out and play rugby for the school teams. They asked me if I would join them, as I had speed and agility on my side, so they believed that I had it in me to be good at it. I was not really into the game of rugby, as I thought it quite senseless to have fifteen men on a side running after a ball simply to kick or to score a try. My father loved rugby, and perhaps this was the reason why I developed apathy for the game. Even from a young age, I was adamant that I would not become what my father would like me to become, I will be nothing like him. This I promised myself over and over again, almost like a chant to ensure that I never become like the loathsome man he was.

But as my friends asked me to join them, I volunteered to try out and see if I would be selected. For try-outs, we had one very strict rugby coach, a Mr van Vuuren, a red-faced burly man who no doubt liked looking down a bottle on regular occasions, who also was a no-nonsense type of guy. The ruddy type, uncouth, stocky and quite abrasive. He was strict and all primary children were quite afraid of *Mister Van*, as he was not so fondly called. Especially when he gave you a hiding, as in those days, corporal punishment was abound and abundant in schools. He took pleasure in punishing boys for any misdemeanour, and many a primary school student prayed not to have Mr Van as his mathematics teacher. I was fortunate enough to skip the wrath of the man during my primary career, as he was not assigned to our class for our math tutoring.

The afternoon of the try-outs all the boys had to follow a set of exercises. Once they passed these fitness exercises, they then were sent a few at a time to Mister Van, who then would take them through a few paces of the game of rugby, letting them kick, run, tackle, pass the ball, get into a line or getting into a scrum position and try to position the ball. Peter and Rudy were in different fitness level as I was, so I was not paired up with them when they had their time with Mister Van.

Both Rudy and Peter made the team, and they jumped for joy. They ran past me just as I was about to be judged for my skills with Mister Van.

"Good luck, mate!" they both shouted at me, on their way to the locker room to hit the showers.

Yeah, right, I thought to myself. A fine pair the two of you are. Asking me to partake and then leaving me once you were selected. Ah, well. I will give it a shot in any event. So the next seven boys were evaluated and we were sent on to Mr Van. As I walked towards him, I noticed Mr Van's face changed, and he took a double look. Very quickly he walked up to me and hissing through his teeth, whispering in a frenzied tone he asked me, "Just where the hell do you think you are going?"

"Sir?" I asked, quite incredulously.

"I am asking you, where the hell do you think you are going and what the hell do you think you are doing?"

"Sir, I am here for the rugby try-outs?"

"What? Are you aware that this is a boy's sport?"

It seemed to me as if it was his turn to be dumbfounded.

"Sir?" I asked, quite unsure of what he could mean.

"Are you aware that this is a sport that is played by boys?" he repeated himself.

"Yes, sir," I answered, not sure if he understood what the game was all about. So much for coaching a game where he was questioning me around who played the game, I thought to myself. But little did I know.

"Are you aware that you can get hurt, that you will be tackled by other boys, thrown to the ground and that they will fight you for the ball?"

"Yes, sir." Again, I was a tad confused by what on earth could he mean.

"Well, I won't have it. I will not have some sissy boy in my team, playing with his limp wrists and running like a faggot, for me to be made the laughing stock of all the other school coaches. My team has no place for faggots. Don't think I do not know what and who you are. You who do the traditional folk dancing, the choir singing, the poem recitals! Go back to your flower garden and faggoty ways and stay away from my rugby team. I will not have you panting over some boy's ass. Now get lost!"

His scathing words reduced me to tears, I turned around, humiliated and ran away, ran as fast as I could to get away from this hateful man. I did not understand what he meant by panting and limp wrists, but I knew once again that the curse of being called a faggot has followed me all the way to the school sports grounds. And being considered a faggot, I was not allowed to try and play a game that was for boys and men only. An outcast, labelled and hated. That was how I felt. When Peter and Rudy, later on, saw me and realised that I had been crying, they accepted that I did not make it in the team and that I was merely disappointed. I could not get myself to tell them that I never even had a chance to try. I quietly allowed them to believe that I simply was not good enough to make the team. And slowly it started to dawn on me that being a faggot was being a boy but not being seen as a boy. Being a boy but not acting like a boy and therefore being despised

165

for not representing what society labelled a boy should be like. A misfit, a boy, yet not a boy in the eyes of the world. And at that age, not older than eleven years, simply unable to understand what needed to change. And instinctively knew that no one at home would tell me what I needed to change or do differently to be a boy.

YOUNG UNREQUITED PUPPY LOVE

From the instance that the realisation dawned on me that I was a freak of nature, that people looked at me differently and opined that I was different to other boys my age, I wanted to make a difference, to be accepted and allowed to be a boy. To lose the label of being called a faggot, which in my mind meant a boy that is not a boy. I didn't know how to be any different to the way that I was, so for the next few years in primary school, I concentrated on the cultural extramural activities at school and my overall academic achievements. I ensured that I never encountered Mr Van where he could humiliate me again, and I often saw him looking at me in a not dissimilar way my father looked at me. Scorn and hate reflected in his eyes, and I was at a loss in understanding what it was about me that made him hate me so much.

During my final year at primary school, a girl that I knew since early school days who was the same age as Sis and in the same grade as Sis caught my eye one day at the public swimming pool, where I spent most summer weekends with Peter and Rudy. Mable was already in high school at this time, but it was as if for the first time I saw her and really liked what I saw. So I started to take notice of her, swimming close to her, chatting with her and having a really great time with her. Peter and Rudy already had girlfriends, and perhaps it was because of them having girlfriends that I was spurred into getting a girl of my own. And Mable seemed to be the right choice.

Mable was seemingly enjoying my attention and the two of us hit it off. Although I have known her since we all were in the same primary school and had several chats with her over the years, something was different this time around. Perhaps it had to do with the fact that I showed an interest in her, and with her encouraging laugh and mutual affection, I was tempted to take her hand, hold her hand while we walked around the swimming pool. And suddenly the boy who was not a boy started to feel like a boy.

So after one particularly hot day at the public swimming pool, I walked Mable home, holding her hand. We talked about trivial things as only two youngsters can do who have a serious case of puppy love. We walked through the local park, quite a distance from the public swimming pools, and we spent some time at the park. The fact that Mable reciprocated my attention made me bold, and so I pecked her on the mouth, innocently, lips pursed and brushed against each other. My heart was pounding in my ears, I was shaking like a leaf, but it felt good. Again, my pursed lips pressed against her pursed lips, all innocently and sweet. Elation coursed through my veins and I remember thinking to myself, so this is what it feels like to be a boy!

We had a primary school dance that was coming up and as Peter and Rudy were excited about taking their girlfriends along, I wanted desperately for Mable to accompany me and be my girlfriend as well. So I mustered all the courage I had and asked her to go to the dance with me.

"I know you are in high school and are older than me, but would you like to go to the dance with me?" I asked.

"When is the dance?" Mable asked. I gave her the date and time.

"Let me think about it, as I will also need to ask my mom," Mable said.

"If you like, I could ask your mom?" I volunteered, as Mable's mom was known to me and she always had a good word for me.

"No, that is quite all right. Let me think about it some, and then I will talk to my mom and let you know, okay?"

"Okay," I agreed and walked Mable to her house.

The next weekend was another scorcher, and again we found ourselves at the public swimming pool. I saw Mable's brothers and sisters there, but Mable was not at the swimming pool. I went to her brother and asked him about where Mable was, and he remembered that he needed to hand me a note from Mable. I thought it odd, went to the men's locker rooms, locked myself in the toilet and read the note from Mable.

> *Hello,*
> *I am so sorry that I am unable to be at the pool today.*
> *Please meet me at the school grounds around four o'clock*
> *this afternoon. I need to talk to you.*
> *Mable*

I rushed to the school grounds, finding Mable waiting patiently for me at one of the swings. I walked up to her to peck her on the cheek and hug her hello, innocently as only two young school children can be, but she held me off with the palm of her hand.

"Please sit down," Mable said to me.

"What is the matter?" I asked.

"I have been having a lot of fun with you lately, and I looked forward to going to the dance with you. But people started talking about me liking you, people in my class, people who were in the same primary school as we were and people who know you."

"I don't understand. What are they telling you?"

"This is hard for me to say, but I think it is best that we are no longer friends."

"Mable? Why? What are they telling you to make you want to react this way?"

"I cannot say the words that they used, but they told me that people are laughing at me for being with you, for holding your hand. Thank God they haven't seen me kissing you."

"Is it because I am younger than you?" I asked.

"No, it is not that. It is because of what you are."

And with those words I realised that despite feeling like a boy, in the eyes of society I would never be a boy, I would always be a faggot. I turned around and walked away, leaving Mable at the school grounds, knowing very well that I would never escape the burden that has burnt such a hole in my soul. That feeling like a boy doesn't make you a boy, doing the things of a boy will not change the way people see you. I needed to change drastically do things very differently but what it was I could not fathom, but I knew that for me to finally be thought of as a boy, a lot of changes would need to be done. What they were, I was oblivious to, but I was not ignorant to the fact that unless I changed, I would always be seen as, labelled as and branded as a faggot.

I did go to the school dance, albeit on my own.

A new girl joined our school a while later, as her parents were forced to move to Tranquillity due to financial commitment strains. Karen was a tall girl, with a dark complexion and black raven hair, but I took a liking to her immediately. I supposed that at this stage, I was adamant that the right thing for a boy to do was to have a girlfriend, but I was also picky and choosy and not any old gal will do! But, I really liked Karen, and as luck would have it, they moved in right next door to where Rudy and his family stayed. Rudy's girlfriend was also close by, so often she would be at Rudy's house, albeit that she was more there for Rudy's sister, playing together than really for Rudy, he was quite chuffed with himself having his girl so close to him. This made me want to spend more time at Rudy's so Peter and I were spending time quite often over there, doing the things that primary boys do, playing and being up to mischief, and taunting the girls. One day we sat outside on the lawn, the three of us, chit chatting when I remarked that I really liked Karen.

"Rudy, as Karen is in our class, have you been talking to her seeing that she is your neighbour and all."

"Yes," Rudy answered me. "She is also a friend of Alma's, so she has been dropping in quite often. She is okay for a girl."

Alma was Rudy's sister who was a year older than Rudy.

"Do you think that if I asked her to go out with me that she would say yes?" I asked.

"How should I know?" he asked me indignantly.

"For heaven sake! You see her here often, surely you have heard her talking about boys to Alma? Has she mentioned my name at all?"

"Not a single word," Rudy said. Peter just smiled, shaking his head at my gall, thinking that perhaps I was mentioned in conversation.

Unbeknownst to us, Alma overheard the conversation and mentioned this in passing to Karen. She did this in front of Karen's bigger brother. He was quite protective of Karen, and the next time I rocked up at Rudy's house, he was waiting for me as well.

"So, are you the scrawny fellow who has a crush on my sister?" he asked me.

I felt the blood rushing to my face, crimson cheeks and dark red patches on my forehead showed him that I was embarrassed by him knowing.

"Ach," I said, "I simply mentioned that I liked Karen," I managed to utter.

"Why is it that you like her?" he asked me.

"He said it is because she has a dark complexion and black crow hair."

Alma had to eavesdrop and then still had the audacity to speak on my behalf and become part of a conversation that she had no invitation to.

"Ach, Alma, I never said that. And I did not say it was a crow's hair, I said it was a raven's hair. There is a difference you know!"

"Ach, ach, ach is all that I hear from you. Are you some kind of faggot?" Karen's brother asked me.

Not again. Please, no, not again. What is it that everyone is seeing in me or hearing from me that I am too blind to see and too deaf to hear? Why is it that people cannot spare your feelings and have to insult you and hurt you in the worst possible sense? Now even in the way I was speaking, people could see that I was a faggot! The only thing that I could do was turn around and stumble away, refusing for Alma to see my defeat and tears. Karen's brother ran after me.

"Hey, little man, I was only joking. Don't worry too much about what I said, hey?" he tried to apologise. For the first time in my life, someone who first called me a faggot afterwards had regrets, although his poor attempt of an apology left much to be desired. The fact that he did say that he was sorry took some of the edges off the terrible pain inflicted on my being, on my soul which again was left in tatters.

I never did pursue Karen, as I simply could not stand knowing what her brother thought of me, despite him saying that he was only joking.

A WOODWORK TEACHER'S LOATHING

As mentioned earlier, I had problems and trouble adapting to high school and for my first year at high school, I chose to be a loner and be on my own. During this time, I went through the custom of attending classes and excelling in my work, but I remained a loner and remained on my own. For the first time in my schooling, I was also to attend a woodwork class. As my father was a carpenter and long dead by this time, I still refused to be anything like him and having to take this compulsory class for the next two years simply filled me with dread. Theoretically, I would excel at the work I told myself, but practically I would not make any effort and trusted that the theoretical part would aid me and assist me in passing the subject. I knew that by the time that I get to standard eight that I would drop this subject like a hot potato, so I had two years where I had to endure, bite the bullet and make the best of it.

The teacher who taught this class was an absolute brute. I disliked him from the first day I saw him. I realised very early on that I had to stay out of his way, as he had a way of picking on children, and he had no qualms about using his flat hand on a boy who did not do what he was supposed to do. Just keep your head down and stay out of harm's way was my motto. However, he was not going to allow me to get away with it. He had a bloodhound's scent, and he immediately could pick up which boys were afraid of him (which was most of the boys in the class), but he had an uncanny way of knowing which ones would make the best and easiest targets. And I was one of them. With absolutely no woodworker or carpentry sense in any fibre of my body, I simply could not grasp the concept of moulding something out of wood. So making a table leg or stool seat or stool leg, all of it required some skill, skill that I never had, as I never had a father who exposed me to tools, and even if he did, with the relationship that we had, I simply would have blundered at it. I was simply terrible at it, to the absolute annoyance and uncanny pleasure of the teacher. He would single me out, take my woodcarvings and show the boys how not to treat wood, how not to carve, how not to cut and how not to create something out of wood. The one day he came from behind, standing silently behind me, watching what I was doing. I was oblivious to his presence, pretending to be busy, praying that the time would go by so that I could leave his dreadful class. The next moment, he slapped me against the back of my head with such force, that my forehead hit the workbench I was sitting at.

"Do you think this is a daydreamer's class where you can sit on your ass and while the time away?" he shouted at me.

"No, sir. I am sorry, sir!" I apologised profusely.

I heard the class starting to snicker. They knew I was in for it. The teacher grabbed the piece of wood that was in my hand and held it up for all to see.

"Look at this masterpiece!" he roared. "I have never seen anything like this. Have you?" he asked the first boy closest to me.

"No, sir!" the boy concurred with the teacher.

He asked several other boys and they all agreed that they have never seen anything like it, all smiling and sniggering at my expense.

The teacher took the piece of wood I was working on, and he threw it on a pile of wood that was in the class, all pieces of wood discarded and no longer in a usable state.

"For your losing your piece of wood, the punishment is severe. You can choose, boy! Either I cane you or you go through a thumping."

"Thumping, thumping, thumping!" the boys in the class all roared. A thumping meant that each boy would get the opportunity to hit me on the butt, kick me on the butt or use a piece of wood on my butt.

"What will it be, boy?" the teacher asked impatiently.

Thinking that the boys would take pity on me and that their punishment would be less painful than that of the teacher's, I opted for a thumping. What a terrible mistake I made. As an outcast, as a loner, the boys seized an opportunity to kick me, beat me and hit me with everything they had in them. Each boy was only allowed one chance, so they made the best of it. My buttocks burned, were bruised and blue by the time the thumping was over.

"Now get your black and blue ass over there and start on your wood from scratch. And we will monitor your progress with keen interest."

As I had no skill whatsoever, I realised I needed a helpline, and as Peter was in the same high school but we drifted apart and albeit that he now was with different and newly made friends, I still felt at ease to ask his assistance. He took my piece of wood, he would work on it and hide it in the class, and when we had to attend class, I would get the worked wood from the hiding place, and to everyone's surprise, it seemed as if I had made some splendid progress. Little did they know.

The day of the slap and the thumping, when I arrived home, my forehead was slightly bruised. Mom noticed this immediately, and with a lot of prompting and prodding, I eventually told her what happened. Mom was livid. The next morning, Mom went to go and see the principal, without my accompanying her, as Mom stated this was an issue that she would handle on her own. Mom never told me what was said, but I could deduce that Mom was no pushover during the meeting she had with the principal and she made her feelings and displeasure known.

The next time we attended the woodwork class, instead of us going to our workbenches, the teacher asked every boy to gather around. We were boys from six different classes that attended the woodwork class together, so we were quite a crowd.

"I believe that a few of you faggots, sissy boys and mommies' boys went to complain to your mommies on how I teach my class," the teacher began.

Not once did he look at anyone other than me, the whole duration of his intimidating speech.

"That many of you are afraid of me, and that I am violent. That I hit you at will, and that I hurt you. You call yourself boys, supposed to grow up to be men. You are mice. You are weak. You are girls running around pretending to be boys. But let me tell you, I have been running this class for the last twenty years, and no faggot, sissy boy or mommy's boy is going to dictate to me on how I should act, react or teach my class. Is that clear?"

Everyone was too afraid to speak.

"Is that clear?" he bellowed.

"Yes, sir," all the boys agreed in unison.

Everyone knew he was talking about me, but the fact that he used the plural made me believe that more than one boy complained. Needless to state, he never lifted his hands against or to me ever again, and in fact, he never so much as spoken a single word with me for the remainder of the time that I spent in his class. He made sure that I received the lowest marks possible on practical, but he could find no fault in my theory. And so I realised, the way I was, the way I spoke, and the fact that I had a mother who stood up for me all made me a faggot. And I was still seeking to find a way of changing to no longer have this hurtful label thrown at me from all directions, unexpectedly and yet ever so often.

THE DAWNING OF A REALISATION

A year later, during my second year of high school, I realised that only I could change the perception that people had of me. So I made a conscious decision to spend more time around men and boys of my own age and less time with Mom and Sis. I believed that this was the only solution to my predicament so that I would be able to get to know the ways of boys and men. That this was the cure for humiliation. So I gradually started to notice a change in behaviour, behaviour towards me, how people, especially boys reacted around me. I was considered less of a freak of nature and more of one of the crowd. This is what I hoped for but also knew that there would still be times that others would consider me as different and that I will probably carry the label with me for the rest of my life. I realised that being with Mom and Sis so often I had some girly ways about me, and this was generally frowned upon by other boys. The more time I spent with boys and the less time I was surrounded by girls, even I realised where I needed to change. That I was a victim of circumstance, that no one was to be blamed for my being different, and once I realised what was 'wrong' in the eyes of society I could change it all and at least in a small way be accepted for who I was, finally.

By the time I was a senior in high school, I fully understood what the meaning of the word faggot was supposed to be. How people could call a young boy this, especially grown-ups like parents and teachers was totally beyond my comprehension. In fact, I stopped trying to understand the ways of man, why it is that we are so hell bent on hurting others that we perceive to be weaker, different or strange to us. For Mom and Sis, this was a tough time to cope with my breaking away, but the bond that existed between us could never be broken. Sure, I still did spend a lot of time with them, but far less than I did in the past and I was seeking independence and manhood, and wanted a role model that epitomised what being a boy or a young man should be. And found this in a few true high school friends, who remained my friends until the end of my high school days, and taught me, unbeknownst to them, how to behave like a boy, act like one and be considered one.

Despite me entering manhood, having true men and lady friends, having relationships with women, falling in love with women, and being considered a man, even today when I hear that word being used in idle conversation or on television I still cringe. It is a word that I would never use, would never utter and never call someone, despite who they are, how they react or what they are labelled as by society. It is a word that inflicts so much pain, suffering and injustice on its recipient that it is a word that should not form part of any vocabulary. People are different, some are strong, others soft, not necessarily weak, and in a world where heterosexuals, homosexuals and trans-gendered all make up parts of society, perhaps we should be more tolerant and accepting that each has a place and a purpose. And that the right to judge any individual based on their differences has never been granted to any mortal being.

***

It has stopped raining, but the day remained cold and bleak. And lying in the bay window, I again felt as strongly as I did as a young man around people ridiculing others for being different. Different does not mean bad. No two people are alike, and not everyone shares the same interests, has the same mannerisms or even the same upbringing. And that people are born the way they are, and that people don't choose to be who they are. That they simply are. And I again realised how much I hated that word, which was meant to hurt, to tear apart, and to destroy. Which was uttered by people who were narrow-minded, who knew no better and who would go through life as bullies, as ignorant and probably very seldom would change their perception, which after all is their own reality. And knowing that I was perceived to be effeminate but spending time with boys and their fathers and having a cognisance of what needed to change, contributed to the crater in my soul caused by the humiliation transformed into a much smaller hole altogether.

5

THE SADDEST HOLE OF ALL – COPING WITH DEATH

DEATH OF A FATHER

For the first nine years of my life, I felt persecuted by a father who had nothing but loathing for me, and one that never could be an idol or role model to me. I loathed my father as much as he loathed me, and we simply never had a relationship. For reasons unknown to me, my father saw me as a weakling, as bad spawn, and the fact that I was nothing like him spurred him on to hate me even more. From ever since I can remember, I hated alcohol and its effect on families and I have first-hand experience of how alcohol can destroy a family, how the very vapours of its destruction resonate with you long after you have survived the destruction. I always knew that I would never touch alcohol, that it was a destroyer, of souls, of families, of unison and of happiness. What I did not realise, was that alcohol was a killer as well. Silently, the grim reaper awaits, as the clutches of alcohol embrace the body it is about to devour. For some, it is a quick reaping, whilst for others, it may be long-suffering. My father fell somewhere smack in the middle of it all.

As I started entering my tenth year, my father got gravely ill. When he finally acquiesced and relented to be taken to a doctor, the prognosis and diagnosis were fatal. From a diagnosis point of view, my father had cirrhosis of the liver, an illness that was caused by his many years of taking to the bottle, to his one true love, his idol and god. In addition to this, due to his liver now no longer being a functional organ, my father also became bloated, literally bloated, as he had retained water as well, which caused him to swell and gain weight at a rapid rate. Pills were prescribed to counter the effect of his ineffectual liver and to slow the build-up of water in his cells and body. Or rather, this was my understanding in the early eighties of my father's illness. The prognosis was dire.

"He only has anything between six months to two years left to live, the doctor told us. His liver was in a most deteriorated state, and there was simply nothing that could be done for him." I overheard Mom speaking to one of her friends.

"What about a transplant?"

"The doctor told us that a liver transplant was indeed possible, but he has to be placed on a waiting list, and time was definitely not on his side. As you know, public healthcare facilities are the last on the list of organ donors. I simply don't know what we will do."

"You will manage," the friend tried to soothe Mom.

My father was also informed that he had one of two choices.

"He could continue drinking and would be dead in six months' time, or he could stop completely and prolong his life, up to a maximum of potentially two years. Knowing him, I don't think he is going to be able to stop drinking."

I realised that Mom was sad and that Mom was very concerned, as somehow to Mom, the thought of going on without my father was more daunting than having a husband guilty of insobriety and debauchery.

"I am simply not able or strong enough to run a household all by myself."

So as the ticking hands of time progressed, Mom got more and more concerned about my father's overall health. Sis was also concerned, as at the tender age of twelve, she realised what death was and always had a fierce love for my father that I could never comprehend, as I most certainly did not feel the same way about him. And my father loved Sis with all his heart, of that much I was certain, as growing up in his house, I could see the love he felt for Sis. Perhaps my father only had it in him to be able to love one child, love that child unconditionally and that it was not so much the fact that he did not love me, perhaps it was that he was incapable of loving me.

I, as an almost ten-year-old child, was totally unperturbed by the sadness and concern that were omnipresent in our family. Granted, I did not understand the finality or the severity of death, I did not understand the meaning of death, I did not understand the suffering my father was going through but one thing I did know at the time was that life for me would be quite more bearable without a father who so humiliated and hated me. So I did not share in any of the feelings that were shown towards my father's condition, and in fact was perceived to be withdrawn.

Although my father did not and could not know how much time, he had left on this mortal soil, from the moment that he found out about his illness and him dying, my father tried to right the wrongs that he inflicted on us as a family. My father's relationship with Mom improved markedly, he took more time to spend with Sis, and he tried to take an interest in me, the boy he used to call a faggot and the one person that was and meant absolutely nothing to him and even worse, was nothing like him. But for me, it was a situation of being too little too late. I continued to avoid him like the plague, as I always used to do in the past whenever he was around, and only answered him when I really needed to. Mom noticed my reluctance to engage with my father and felt it her duty to address the situation with me.

"My child, you do realise that your father is quite sick?" she asked me the one day after another futile attempt by my father to have a spontaneous conversation with me.

"Yes, Mom, I know that he is ill," I answered.

"Do you know what the meaning of death is?" Mom asked.

"Yes, Mom. It is similar to what happened to Nana and to Tippy," I answered. Nana was my maternal grandmother and Tippy was Mom's beloved dog, whom we all loved dearly.

"My son. He is your father. And in this world, you only ever get one father. And in the end, it doesn't matter if he was a good or a bad person. What matters is what he was in the days before he died. You can see that he is trying; he wants to talk to you and wants to know that you are okay. Your father is dying, my child. He doesn't have a lot of time left on this earth and each day that he wakes up is a blessing from a merciful God. He is trying to say he's sorry, in his own awkward way. He wants to get to know you better. He now has some time, and he spends this time trying to get to know you and Sis better. Let him, child. Please, do not shut him out. For if you do, and he should die, you will live with the regret for the rest of your life."

I simply could not do it. I heard and tried to understand what Mom was saying to me, but I simply did not trust my father to be a nice caring person where it concerned me. I could not for one moment let my guard down, for the moment I did, and he attacked again with his abusive and foul words, he would simply rip me apart, tear me to pieces. Even at the age of ten, I knew that I could not open my heart, soul and mind to the one person that I desperately wanted to open it up for. I was simply too afraid. He had mentally kicked me once too many times with the slurs he hauled at me, that I was consequently too wary and weary to allow him anywhere near me emotionally.

My father never stopped trying in the final year of his life since his diagnosis, and for Mom's sake, I did engage a few times but in simple and trivial discussions of no importance or consequence at all. Just to also get Mom off my back with her constant whining that I will regret my actions once my father has died.

"So how is school?" my father asked me the one afternoon.

"School is fine," I obligingly answered.

"Do you find any subjects to be difficult that you need some help with?"

"Not really."

"Do you have any friends at school?"

"Yes."

"So why don't I ever see them coming around."

"I go to them sometimes," I answered him.

One late Tuesday afternoon in early July, my father had the need to use the corrugated iron toilet that was in the backyard of our house in Tranquillity. And after using the toilet as my father stood up, big and bloated as a result of the illness and the water in his body, he had a sharp pain in his chest, which caused him to fall over and out through the toilet door. The impact of him hitting the concrete floor must have somehow contributed towards him surviving his first heart attack, albeit that he was bruised as a result of the direct impact he had with the floor.

Mom witnessed my father's unfortunate incident, ran to him and managed with her tiny body to drag him up, this huge bloated man who outweighed her three times. Tears were running down Mom's cheeks, but she managed and my father gained his consciousness through all this.

"Oh, dear Lord!" Mom cried. "Look at your face. You have hurt yourself falling. What happened?"

My father was unable to explain to Mom other than to let her know that he had a sharp chest pain and lost his balance.

Mom immediately took my father into the room, as she wanted him to lie down on the bed. She then sent Sis to our neighbours to ask them to call the doctor. Sis was in tears, very concerned about what had happened to my father.

As Mom helped my father entering the room taking him to their bed, my father had a second heart attack, falling face forward on the bed, both his hands clutching at his chest again. With a huge crash, my father almost broke the bed with the impact of him falling, and again he somehow managed to resuscitate his heart.

Mom at this time frantically asked our neighbours to call the local doctor in Tranquillity again, who was familiar with my father's condition and who arrived within ten minutes of receiving the first call. After attending to my father, the doctor immediately called for an ambulance and told Mom that my father had to be admitted to hospital as a matter of urgency. The doctor also declared that my father had survived two severe heart attacks and that a third one could be massive and fatal, and hence had to be taken to hospital immediately to get the necessary care and proper treatment.

The ambulance arrived within thirty minutes after the doctor summoned them to our house, and by this time, most of Mom's friends were there to give Mom the support she required. How they heard about what happened, I will never know, but somehow it spread like a wildfire.

The medics wanted to carry my father on a stretcher, but he refused, stating that he was fine and that he would get into the ambulance by himself. My father managed to walk very slowly out of the house, managed to walk to the ambulance, and was able to get into the ambulance himself. Before my father got into the ambulance, he turned around and said goodbye to everyone who was present. He then asked Sis to come and give him a kiss goodbye and when he was done with hugging and kissing her, he called me to give me a kiss goodbye as well. I walked up to my father, and for the first time in my life since I could remember, my father kissed me on the cheek. Without a further word, he turned around and got into the ambulance. Mom and her one best friend got in the ambulance with my father, and her other best friend was to follow the ambulance to the hospital to return Mom and her friend once my father was admitted to hospital. Ten minutes into the trip to the hospital, my father suffered massive cardiac arrest, and died in the ambulance.

By the time Mom and her friends returned from the hospital, as Mom still had to take care of some formal details, the remaining friends who had stayed behind to look after Sis and I immediately could sense on Mom's distraught face that my father had passed away. Sis was hysterical and everyone was crying around me. The sadness and heartache were palpable. I was sad, sad for Mom, sad for Sis, and sad for the people who were crying around me. But I could not find or muster a single thread of sadness for my father's passing. And as we sat there that Tuesday evening, with Dallas airing on the TV, its end tune playing, friends and family members gathered for support. I recall that to fill the time between programs the SABC played a song on the TV. The song was "Give me back my love". This song had everyone going and afterwards, Mom asked one of her friends to rather switch off the television, as she simply was unable to cope with everything taking place.

The next couple of days were filled with arrangements for the funeral, and Mom decided to keep Sis and me from going to school. In between, family and friends took turns spending as much time with Mom and us as to ensure that we coped during this time of mourning. Mom had to buy appropriate clothes for the family to attend the funeral and she had to pay all the funeral expenses as well, as no provision was made at all for the death of a loved one. My father also never worked at any one company long enough to build up a substantial pension and in fact, the last year of his life he was unemployed and what little money there was left from his working days was used for normal household expenses. Mom, therefore, had nothing that would support us as a family into the future and had to use the money from the Fafi and some contributions made by her friends towards my father's funeral. Sis was extremely sad during this time, and Mom believed that she had to be strong for both our sakes. Mom was so busy taking care of arrangements during this time that her time for grief only happened in the evenings. Grieving for a husband who was no more. A man Mom loved from the first day she set eyes on him and who in the beginning of their courtship years had made her so very happy. I heard Mom crying almost silently during the evenings during her time of grief, and I believe that her friends and family carried her through during her time of mourning.

On the morning of my father's funeral, I went to Mom to tell her that I was grappling with a problem.

"Mom, I am afraid for today," I started.

"What are you afraid of, my son?" Mom asked.

"Mom, I am afraid that I will be unable to cry today at the funeral."

I did not have a true understanding of what funerals were all about but knew enough that it was a place where people cried for the loss of a loved one.

"Of course you will cry!" Mom said slightly exasperated. "He was your father after all."

"Mom, I know. But I also know how I am feeling inside. I cannot find any sadness inside me Mom. I see Sis cry, I see the people who knew him cry. I hear you cry. But Mom, I have not cried, and I have never felt like crying."

"You are holding back your feelings, that's all," Mom said. "Let it go. Cry for the death of your father. Cry for the fact that you will never see him again."

"Mom, please don't get angry with me, but how can I cry for something like that, when that was what I always wanted my whole life. To never see him again."

"Stop it! You just stop it!" Mom was shocked at my revelation. I was dumbfounded, as I could not understand how it was that Mom did not know how I felt. We lived in the same house, she saw and noticed how I avoided spending any time with my father, how I never even wanted to engage in any conversation with him. It must be the grief, I told myself. Mom was longing for my father and therefore could not see things as they were. But I knew I had to go on and I had to say what needed to be said, even at that young and tender age.

"Mom, I am sorry. But what am I going to do? I know I am not going to cry and I don't want people coming up to me and saying things to me. I know they will be worried, Mom. And I cannot tell them what I am telling you now."

"Oh child, the Lord must help me today. If what you are saying is true, if you are not feeling an ounce of sadness for the passing of your father, then for appearance's sake, look down and when people talk to you, look sad. I don't want people to think that you are in need of help. That you are traumatised and cannot cope with the loss of your father. So keep your head down the whole time during the funeral procession."

Mom quickly prayed and I knew she felt sick to her stomach on top of her grief to provide me with such unwise yet sound advice at the same time. But I knew that doing what Mom suggested would not be good enough. I am ten years old, for heaven's sake. How will people believe me, they are adults after all. So I decided the only way I could do this and get through this day without adding additional strain on Mom, was to take an onion and place it in a plastic bag and keep the plastic bag in my jacket pocket. Once we leave for the funeral, I would remove the onion and reseal the plastic bag, and hopefully, it would retain enough of the onion's odours that would make my eyes burn and cry at the same time.

Before we got out of the courtesy car of mourning, which was provided to the family as part of the funeral procession, I looked into the bag. My eyes stung like crazy and immediately started watering, tears running down my eyes. It burnt like nothing I ever felt in my life and I started crying for real, as the pain in my eyes was excruciating.

When we walked into the church, the family entered first, my father's coffin was at the entrance of the church. My father had an open casket. This proved to be too much of an ordeal for Sis, who grabbed hold of my father, crying hysterically, kissing my father's brow and holding his head in her hands. I did not have the courage to glance at my father's corpse and as I walked slowly into the church, I again felt the sadness that was around me. And realised that my father played a huge role in Sis' life and that Mom loved him right to the end. That their pain and hurt were almost unbearable for them and that they did not know how they were going to get through this terrible ordeal. I was also saddened again in church and at the gravesite that I was unable to mourn for the man who fathered me. I was unable to forgive him for the pain and suffering he inflicted on my psyche over all those years. If anything, I never needed to prove myself to him again and fail at it. No one, except for Mom and Sis around me knew the true extent of my feelings. As this was a private family issue, no one needed to know. Not then. Not ever.

***

I have never returned to my father's grave and to this date do not know the exact location of where he was buried. More than three decades later, and the impact he had on my life and how it turned out had been significant and quite substantial, as proving him wrong was the driving force behind every decision and success and even failures I had in life. But I know now, growing up not having a father is possibly one of the most lonely and difficult things a boy can and must endure going from boyhood, to teenager into manhood. I had no one that I could talk about when it came to advice, especially dealing with the hormonal changes boys go through when they go through adolescence and puberty. But mostly, when I looked at my friends and their relationships with their fathers, I also knew that I never had the opportunity to have a true father figure, nor a father as a friend. That card, life was not prepared to have dealt to me. And my soul was poorer for the lack of having a father who could also have been a friend and confidante.

Standing in the kitchen, drinking a cup of hot chocolate and reliving the past again, I realised that for many years my soul could never heal on one specific hole that was carved, and that was the hole of a father not being present. Not even when he was alive. And I came to the realisation that I never forgave my father, that I also only spoke of him with hatred the very few times I needed to talk about him. That I never thought of him, but somehow, deeply and sub-consciously I always blamed my father. Hated him. Despised him. And that today has some significance to me. Today is exactly the day that my father passed away thirty-five years ago. And on this day, I have finally been able to reconcile with my father in my heart and in my soul. And that on this day, with the dream, with the song and with the anniversary date of his passing, I finally could let go of the hatred, of the desolation, of the rejection. That my soul can heal this one hole almost entirely and that I am able to say, "Father, I for-give you."

"I have been thinking of getting a dog," I said to Mom one day. "We have a very nice home now, a big backyard, a pool and it, therefore, is big enough for quite a big dog as well."

"Who will look after the dog and who will clean up after it?" Mom enquired.

"We will all look after the dog, Mom. She will be our little treasure."

"What about Sasha?" Mom enquired, concerned that the poodle that Mom had for the last ten years would be in danger.

"If we get a pup, Mom, she will grow up with Sasha and they will become instant friends. You will see that they will bond."

Mom loved Sasha with her dear heart and would protect Sasha until the very end.

"You just make sure that Sasha is kept out of harm's way. The first time I smell trouble, the dog must go."

"Relax, Mom. Sasha will be fine."

"You know she does not make friends with other dogs quite easily."

"Mom, she is a house dog in any event. These days she hardly walks in the garden and she does all her ablutions in the front garden, in any event, so she will not be in the backyard where we will keep the other dog."

"What is it with you that you now want another dog?" Mom asked incredulously.

"I have been wanting a companion for a while now, Mom. And a bigger dog will also give us the protection we need. There are days that you don't feel up to travelling and going to Tranquillity, and these are the days that the dog would be a comfort and protection for you."

"Who will feed her?" Mom asked.

"Before work, I will give her food and when I return from work I will replenish her food again."

I realised that Mom was not against me getting a dog, but she was gravely concerned about Sasha and how Sasha would adapt with a new dog in the house. But the issue was settled and I set out to getting a dog. And the breed I always loved is an Alsatian, or German Shepherd. They are very loyal, very protective and they have a special disposition and kind nature.

I scanned the newspapers, went to pet shops, and finally found someone who was breeding German Shepherds. After negotiating the best possible price for the dog, one Sunday morning a girl friend of mine and I went to go and pick up the dog, as Sis was unable to do so on this day.

When we arrived at the breeder's home, there was a litter of a few pups. We could choose any from that specific litter, the breeder advised us. Looking at all five the pups, who all were eager for attention, there was only one female in the litter, and she pulled at my heartstrings immediately. So naturally, she was the one that I selected.

"The female please." I pointed out to the breeder.

"Planning on breeding with her?" he asked.

"No, I will ensure that she is fixed. We do not want to breed at all," I said.

The breeder then gave me a box and we placed the tiny dog in the box, ready for our journey to return home. The dog disliked the movement of the car intensely and vomited all over herself in the box. I was very close to getting sick myself, and the journey home felt endless. When we finally arrived at home, I immediately cleaned the tiny pup and introduced her to Sasha. As expected, Sasha simply wanted nothing to do with this new creature that was invading her space and family. She simply ignored the pup. The pup, on the other hand, was not as obliging and was followed Sasha around, squealing, crying, biting, and barking at Sasha the whole time. Sasha would have none of it and simply jumped onto the sofa, where she knew the pup could not reach her. And promptly fell asleep, despite the mewling that came from the pup.

As I did not want the pup to become used to being indoors, I took the pup outside and played with her. I was concerned that the pup would fall into the pool, despite us having a safety net, as the pup was very tiny and could easily fall through the holes in the net. So I tried to show the pup the dangers of getting close to the pool. After spending quite some time with the pup, I was exhausted, and while lying on the grass, I fell asleep. The pup cuddled up to me, lying in the folds of my arm, and fell asleep with me. This was the start of a wonderful bond between Coco and me.

That evening, leaving Coco outside, I erected a fence between the pool and the yard as to ensure that Coco could not get close to the pool. What a dilemma and catastrophe! Coco simply did not want to be alone or apart from the rest of us, and she cried into the early hours of the morning. Finally fed up with the ruckus that took place, Mom and Sis promptly instructed me to let Coco sleep in the house for the evening else she would wake the entire neighbourhood if she had not done so already. So I went outside, took Coco in my arms, who immediately started licking my face with that stale pup breath! I took her inside, looked for her box, closed my room door, switched off the light and thought that this would be a signal for Coco that she was now safe and could fall into a slumber. But dear Coco had other plans. She was wide-awake and wanted to play. I was dead tired but had to indulge her, or else she created a commotion that would keep Mom and Sis awake. Eventually, she fell asleep, as did I. Far too soon the next morning I had to wake up and leave for work.

After feeding Coco, I again placed her behind the makeshift fence as to ensure that she was safe. Mom was staying at home and reluctantly promised to keep an eye on Coco. And so a ritual started for the next week or so, with Coco growing, crying at night, taken inside and playing a bit and then falling asleep. The first week of getting a new pup, I hardly had any sleep and had my regrets, but knew that it was only temporarily.

A few weeks later, I took down the makeshift fence and allowed Coco to roam freely in the yard. This was to become her domain, albeit that she did not mind sharing it with Sasha. Sasha on the other hand barely tolerated Coco and would growl and snarl at Coco if Coco came too close to her. Coco never minded and by this time, she had outgrown Sasha. But she was very accepting of Sasha. And after I took down the fence, it was also the first evening that we would attempt to let Coco sleep outside, as there simply was no more time to delay the inevitable. And I did not hear a sound from Coco. So quiet was it outside that I had a fright that she may have fallen in the pool somehow. As the window in my room overlooked the pool, I was at the window constantly to make sure that Coco was fine. I needn't have worried, Coco was patrolling and playing and enjoying the freedom of the entire yard, but somehow also was aware of the dangers of getting close to the pool.

Coco. Her name was chosen for a specific reason, as she was a blend of cocoa and tan colours. With the most beautiful brown piercing eyes that looked deep into your soul. Every evening after work, I could not wait to get out of my work clothes, dressed in my tee-shirt and shorts and out into the yard I would go. And once she heard the door opened, there was simply no need to call her name. She came bouncing and hopping along, always glad to see me, always ready to greet me in her own special way. She would jump up, lick my face, give me her paw and then expected a belly rub, and it had to be a long rub as she simply adored lying on her back having her tummy rubbed, all four legs in the air. Sheer bliss. By this time, Mom and Sis have both grown to adore Coco almost as much as I did, albeit that Sasha still kept her distance and still pretended to be the alpha female of our household.

And without noticing it, time passed and Coco was with us for an entire year already. By this time, she had grown to her full size and what a formidable lady she was. She was a proud dog, ingrained as part of her heritage and she allowed no stranger on our property. If friends came to visit, we had to first make sure that she got acquainted with them, else she simply would not allow them into our backyard. She somehow sensed that we were fine with them around us, and only then would she tolerate them and even at times once she got to know them better, allow them to play with her as well. By this time, she often also spent time with me in the pool, and I was simply amazed at how much she loved the water. Even during winter, we would often hear her jump onto the first step of the pool, lapping up the water and standing in the freezing cold water. This behaviour was beyond me, but this was part and parcel of who Coco was.

A little after having Coco for fourteen months, I received a distressing call from Mom one morning at work.

"I think Coco has died." Mom sobbed in my ears.

I went cold, ice cold, numb in fact. This is simply not true, cannot be happening, Mom must be mistaken. But then I thought she somehow got out and may have been bumped by a car.

"Did she get out?" I asked Mom frantically.

"No," Mom said between sobs. "She was barking at someone who walked past, then she started walking funny and then she collapsed, lying on the step behind the kitchen door."

This simply is impossible, I thought. She is only almost fifteen months old. Surely she could not have collapsed.

What I did not realise is that Mom called Sis first, and as we both worked for the same company in the same building. Sis arrived on my floor, with tears streaming down her face.

"Mom is mistaken," I croaked. "But we have to go there in case Coco needs to go to the vet."

So Sis and I left work and returned home, the entire journey trying to rationalise why Mom could have been mistaken. But when we arrived home, and I called for her, there was no one to greet me. No jumping, no hopping, no tummy rub. A feeling of utter despair took hold of me, choked me and threatened to overwhelm me.

"Where is she?" I cried. "Where is she, Mom?" I shouted through tears.

Mom led the way, and that is how we found Coco, lying on her side, on the step, her eyes closed. But not a sound and not a breath came from her.

O dear God no. Please dear God no. Please let this not be true, I prayed to myself. But I realised that Coco was gone. My Coco. My best friend. My confidante. My companion. My Coco who accepted me unequivocally and unconditionally.

My entire world was falling apart. I was wailing. It was as if I lost my own child. The hurt stuck in my throat and I struggled to swallow. I did not want to be consoled. I wanted to be alone with Coco. For how long I was like that, I am unsure but sometime later Mom and Sis finally managed to break through my invisible fence and I succumbed to their consoling and comforting me.

After a while, still crying I realised that we had to take action as Coco could not be left like this.

"We need to wrap her in a blanket," I said. "Then we need to take her to the vet. I need to know what the cause of her death was."

Mom went inside and took one of our best blankets, and Sis and I wrapped Coco in the blanket. We then picked her up, and we carried her to my car. We drove the three kilometres to the vet, and upon arriving at the vet, we were immediately assisted.

"I am not sure what happened," I tried explaining to the vet, all the time with tears running down my eyes. "But my mom said she simply collapsed. I don't know if she was poisoned or what the cause was, but please could you do the necessary to find out what happened?"

The vet then explained that Coco would have to be sent to an area in the north where they do autopsies on animals and that I would not be able to retrieve her remains, as these were the rules. They wanted to hand back the blanket to us, and my request was that if I cannot get her remains, and if they were going to dispose of the body after the autopsy was done, that they dispose of the blanket as well. This was the last act of love that I could bestow on my best friend ever. And my soul was destroyed. Utterly desolate. I had no words and I simply could not believe that my Coco had died, that she had left me, that she was gone.

Sis and I returned to work, both with heavy hearts. How I got through that day I will never know. But I felt that my whole world was falling apart. As if the rug was pulled from underneath me. And I simply did not know how I was going to muster the energy to continue. As this was the single biggest loss I have experienced in terms of death. And I felt that I was simply not geared to cope with it.

Unbeknownst to me, Sis had called Linda and told her of my loss. At this stage, Linda and I just started our friendship, and she came over with her two kids, and they simply sat with me, while I was lying on the carpet in our lounge, my head resting on my arms and tears dripping on the carpet. Words were superfluous, but their presence made my loss a little bit easier to carry.

***

Coco died more than twenty years ago and to this day, I will never forget her. We did find out what the cause of her death was, she was born with a defective heart. The doctors were amazed and surprised by the fact that she lived for fourteen months, as the symptoms of her defective heart included some severe hot spells as well. I could only believe that the reason why she was in the pool as often as she was had to do with her way of cooling herself. Coco came into my life for but a very brief period of time. But on this cold and bleak and dreary winter's day, the day that all the holes in my soul made me walk down memory lane, Coco's memory has never and will never fade. Coco whose death caused a part of my soul to die, a part that could never ever become alive again. And will never heal. And will never become whole again.

A MATRIARCH IS CALLED TO HEAVEN

Over the years, Mom has started to show the signs of living a brutal life. A life of poverty, of strife and a life where she had to contend with knowing that my father was a drunkard, an abusive husband and someone who could not provide on a continuous basis for his family. That she constantly lived a life in fear, fear that she might be caught for her illegal gambling game, fear that there will not be food for her children and most of all, fear that her children may be taken away from her if she was unable to provide for them. Each line in Mom's face, deeply etched, was a line testament to and caused by living such a brutal and hellish life. That Mom never had it great or easy in life and that her biggest joy, her biggest triumphs and her biggest achievements to her were having Sis and I. And proud she was no doubt, albeit that she had very little understanding of the work that we do. She only knew that both Sis and I never needed for anything in life since started working and progressing in our careers.

With us no longer staying in Tranquillity, but with Mom having her friends and family still in Tranquillity, we lived up to the promise to have Mom dropped off in the mornings with either a friend or at my aunt's, and then on the way home we would pick Mom up again. There were times that Mom did not want to go and visit and on these days, Mom stayed behind at our home. But Mom never went anywhere without her faithful companion, her little poodle, Sasha.

One day whilst visiting my aunt again in Tranquillity, Sasha, who by this time has reached the tender age of sixteen years already, was wandering in my aunt's garden, when a stray dog brutally attacked Sasha and almost tore her apart. Mom was the first to react, as she later recounted the ordeal. Mom knew that Sasha's life was in her hands and she had to act. So Mom got in between the fight, grabbed hold of the stray, kicked it, tore at it, hit at it, all in an effort to make the stray let go of Sasha. When Mom's attack was too much to bear, the stray tossed Sasha aside and made a run for it.

"You must come; you need to take Sasha to the vet now! If you don't come now, she will never make it! My precious Sasha will die!" Mom wailed over the phone after she got hold of me.

I immediate got in my car, raced to my aunt's house and we then took Sasha to the vet. Sasha was a dear little fighter, but her life was hanging by a thread.

"This does not bode well for Sasha," the vet advised us. "Not only has she been terribly torn and brutalised, but her age is also counting against her."

"Please do everything you can to save my dearest Sasha," Mom pleaded with the vet.

Three hours later the vet finished with his operation on Sasha and advised us that she was in critical but stable condition. The next twenty-four hours would be crucial and would be indicative if Sasha would pull through or not. But Sasha was a fighter, and the next afternoon when we returned to the vet's consulting rooms, we were pleasantly surprised at the progress made by Sasha. She was awake, she was sore and we had to handle her with care, as she was quite fragile. Mom was elated, and she stayed at home for the next couple of weeks, making sure that Sasha was taken care of and that she was given proper time to heal and recuperate.

The attack on Sasha, however, took its toll, and a year after the attack, sadly, our little fighter who was with us for so many years, and who was so attached to Mom passed away in her sleep. Mom was inconsolable, and for many weeks after Sasha's passing, Mom simply could not cope with the death of her little poodle. We had Sasha cremated, and Mom kept the box of ashes on her dressing table, next to a photo of Mom and Sasha. Mom would continue to pine for Sasha, and I so very well understood Mom's grief and loss, as I went through something very similar with losing Coco.

Mom continued to have regular visits to Tranquillity, and it was tough in the beginning for Mom to visit friends and family without Sasha by her side. Eventually, Mom adapted, although she never truly got used to it as her visits became more frequent.

Over the years, Mom became more fragile. One particularly cold and brutal winter, Mom's health started to deteriorate, as she had a very bad cough and we asked her to stay indoors. But Mom was stubborn and insisted that she was fine.

"It is winter, Mom," Sis admonished Mom.

"And there is not enough heat where you are visiting and it is going to make things worse," I said to Mom.

"I will be fine. I will stay indoors under a blanket. But I am not staying at home alone," Mom has made up her mind.

So we dropped Mom off that morning, and during the day I phoned my aunt to find out how Mom was doing. Mom was still coughing badly my aunt informed me and suggested that Mom slept over.

"Is Mom okay with sleeping over and us not picking her up?" I asked my aunt.

"She is fine; I have already spoken to her so she knows that you are not picking her up tonight. She has agreed that the cold air would not be good for her so it is best that she stayed inside," my aunt said.

"Please look after her and please let us know if she needs any-thing," I asked. "Also, please make sure that she eats, as she hasn't had an appetite since she started becoming sick. Do you need anything, any groceries that we could supply?"

"Yes, please," my aunt answered me. "That way I can make her some soup."

So on the way home, we first stopped and bought some groceries and supplies for my aunt, dropped it off, looked in on Mom who was asleep and looked fine to us. But both Sis and I were quite concerned about Mom's health.

The next morning I dropped Sis off at the hospital, as she had to undergo a knee operation and I told her that I would look in on her during the evening. I then left for work. Later on that morning, I phoned my aunt who told me that Mom was asleep, that she only woke up for a few minutes, but did not have anything to eat as yet since we dropped her off the previous morning. I was even more concerned now and decided to drive to my aunt and see how Mom was doing.

When I arrived at my aunt's, I was in total shock. Between seeing my Mom the previous evening and seeing her this morning, she had deteriorated quite substantially. I was annoyed with my aunt for not being able to see that my Mom has gone worse. Without a word, I picked Mom up and I carried her to my car. Mom was completely unaware of it, she was totally out cold. I strapped Mom in, and I drove as fast as I could to the hospital. At the hospital, after parking the car, I left Mom in the car who up to this stage had not shown any signs of consciousness. I went looking for a wheelchair, I found one, returned to the car, took Mom out of the car and placed and seated her in the wheelchair. I then hurried Mom in the wheelchair to the Emergency section, where the nurse took one look at Mom and all hell broke loose. Mom was admitted immediately to the high care unit of the hospital where she was given oxygen and the doctors tended to her. When the doctors finally arrived to speak to me, they told me that

Mom had double pneumonia and that if we had waited any longer, Mom would not have made it and that she would possibly had succumbed to her illness. Mom was weak and dehydrated and she needed care. I felt guilty, as although we insisted that Mom went to the doctor, as Mom was stubborn, we allowed her to persuade us that she was fine. I would never be able to live with myself if through sheer negligence we would lose our mother, I told and blamed myself.

As I was unable to see Mom for quite some time, I went to look Sis up who already had her operation done. Sis was in a wheelchair as well, and when she saw me at the hospital she immediately knew that something was wrong.

"What is it?" she asked. "Why are you here now?"

I relayed the incident with Mom and told her that Mom had been admitted and was in high care now. Sis started to cry and she also felt guilty that we allowed Mom to dissuade us from seeking medical assistance.

Whilst still talking to Sis, the receptionist at the hospital called me aside and mentioned that she had something to discuss with me.

"Please, could we have your mother's medical aid details as we attended to her emergency first before taking care of the administrative duties."

"My mother does not have any medical aid," I responded.

"Then how will the bill be settled?" the receptionist enquired.

"I will be paying the account."

"We would need one hundred thousand rand upfront to keep your mother in high care." The receptionist advised me.

I felt the blood draining from my face. One hundred thousand rand. I simply did not have that kind of funds on hand or available.

"I am sorry. But we do not have that kind of money. What options are available to us?"

"I could speak to the doctor and see if we could move your mother to the intensive care unit. If so, we would need twenty-six thousand rand from you."

"I am able to come up with twenty-six thousand rand. Please, could you find out from the doctor if this is not going to put my mother's life in jeopardy? For if we need to, we will get a loan from the bank."

The receptionist spoke to the doctor who after attending to my mother one more time advised us that my mother could be moved to the intensive care unit. I was then able to put the deposit down, thankful that we at least had some funds available to be able to take care of Mom. The doctor also told me that Mom was awake and that we could briefly look in on her.

When Sis and I went into the intensive care unit and looked in on Mom, she was, however, asleep again, but I could see the change in her brought on by the medical care she received. And I felt hugely relieved. I realised that during this whole ordeal I was silently praying to the Lord to please heal Mom, to not take her away from us yet and to guide her and keep her during this time. And the Lord answered my prayers. And I could not thank the Lord enough. Over and over I said thank you and was very glad that Mom was fine.

As there was nothing else that I could do and was not allowed to stay with Mom indefinitely, Sis and I agreed that I would return to work and as she was recovering from her operation, she was in the same hospital so she would look in on Mom every now and then. In all this, I never once asked Sis how she was doing, but she understood that we had such a fright with Mom's illness. She did, however, tell me that she had some discomfort but fortunately, she did not have a lot of pain. I returned to work with the promise that I will be at the hospital that evening during visiting hours again.

That evening when I arrived at the hospital, Mom was already transferred to a general ward, where she was constantly on oxygen but fully conscious. When I walked into the ward, I was overwhelmed by how well Mom has recovered, all within a matter of hours. All with the grace of God, I thought to myself. Mom was a bit confused, perhaps due to all the oxygen, but otherwise, she was alert and fine. Yes, she still had a cough and the pneumonia was being treated, but if all things went well, Mom would be released from the hospital in a week's time.

"Don't you just like what I have done with my room?" Mom asked me, in the confused state that she was in.

"I love it, Mom," I indulged Mom.

"I was not talking to you, my son. I was talking to Sophie," Mom admonished me. But I was the only one in the room?

Mom continued to have her conversation with Sophie until Sis wheeled herself into the ward, whereby Mom then for the first time that evening focused on both of us. Mom was totally oblivious of Sis being in a wheelchair and simply continued having a conversation with us around trivial things. But we both felt enormously relieved by Mom's progress and hence did not mind the tiny delirious state she was in.

Halfway through visiting hours, a nurse came up to us.

"The doctor has requested whether you would be able to meet with her tomorrow at 10:00?"

As Sis was in hospital for her knee operation there was no problem for her to be there, and I simply arranged with work to for that morning work from home first and then go into the office later on.

The next morning, both Sis and I met the doctor in her consulting room. She ushered us in promptly at 10:00.

"Please have a seat," the doctor said to me as Sis was still in her wheelchair. "Your mother has been very fortunate in that you brought her to hospital in time. I reiterate and re-emphasise the fact that it is critical to ensure that older and our more senior of citizens are cared for especially this time of year."

"Sorry, Doctor," I interrupted. "We do care very well for our mother, however, we did not realise the extent of her illness." I defended our actions.

"No, no, I am sorry," the doctor answered. "What I meant was that I understand how stubborn older people are and how they hate coming to hospitals, as they always associate hospitals with death. But that the transformation from bronchitis to pneumonia can happen overnight and therefore they need to be watched and cared for more than normal. But this is not the reason why I called you here. We have done a number of tests on your mother yesterday, and our prognosis is not good. We have detected that your mother also has cancer."

"We are aware of the cancerous growth against my mom's head, but we had been to a doctor before and albeit that it is skin cancer, it is not malignant as per the doctor."

"I am not referring to your mother's skin cancer. Your mother also has cancer of the stomach."

Both Sis and I were totally floored. Mom had never indicated any signs of being in pain or not eating or not being able to keep her food in. We voiced this concern with the doctor.

"Your mother's cancer is not the type that causes her to have pain or to not retain her food intake. However, in order to ensure that we prevent the spread of cancer, we recommend that we operate to remove the cancerous tumour and then have your mother treated to prevent any further spread. From the look of it, your mother has had this cancer for a while now, and the rate of growth and spread is very slow, but it, therefore, makes for imperative and immediate action."

"Doctor," I said. "My mother has always been quite adamant that she would never allow her to be cut opened and any cancer or tumour removed. She has always felt that the moment you cut her open, that is the moment that she will start dying. We simply cannot go against her wishes. I am sure that this cancer that you have detected has not grown overnight and must have been there for quite some time now."

"I really don't think it is your decision to make. I decided to speak to you first as your mother is still recovering from her pneumonia, but I was planning on talking to her once she has recovered and I feel she is up to having the discussion."

"I am sorry, Doctor, but I disagree. It is, in fact, our decision to make. Our wishes are that you will not under any circumstances have the right or the authority to speak to my mother about any cancer. She has been living with this for quite some time now, based on your facts, oblivious of this. I will not hasten my mother's death by letting her know that she has cancer. And for the record, I forbid anyone to speak to my mother about this. We will as a family deal with this and address it at the right and appropriate time."

With that said, both Sis and I left the doctor's consulting room. We both knew that we were honouring Mom's decision and we also knew that the moment that Mom was told, that she would give up. She simply would not have the strength to fight this. Her biggest fear, besides dying alone, was to have cancer and on many occasions, she would remind us that she would never go for an operation to be cut opened and then to have the cancer spread and to die suffering. And she made us promise that we would honour this wish of hers. This was a very tough decision to make, but one that we knew if we had to make it, that we were bound to respect Mom's wishes, no matter how hard it was for both of us. And we solemnly made a commitment to each other to never let anyone know, in the unlikely event that someone may mention it to Mom. Not knowing, we rationalised, was far better than knowing, as when the mind knows, then the mind gives up and eventually the body follows.

I left for work and told Sis that I would return that evening at visiting hours. Driving to work, I was in emotional turmoil, that the tempest and tsunamis of feelings and emotions that went through my mind and my body threatened to overwhelm me. But there was one light at the end of this dark tunnel. If the cancer was not painful, and if Mom could retain her food intake and if the spread is so very slow as we were made to understand from the discussion with the doctor, then Mom may still have many a happy year with us without treatment and suffering and pain. And that became my consolation, my belief and my conviction. Somehow, with this thought in mind, I felt peace.

That evening I returned to the hospital, and Mom was her old self again.

"Who gave you the permission to bring me and have me admitted to hospital?" Mom scolded me as I walked in and kissed her on the cheek to greet her.

"If we did not do it, you would have died," I retorted.

"That is utter nonsense. I was fine; I only had a bad case of the flu."

"Mom, you have double pneumonia. Ask the doctor. We brought you in just in time. If we waited one more day, it would have been too late."

"I don't care or believe it. Get me out of here. I want to go home," Mom argued.

"You are not going anywhere until you have recovered fully," I argued back with Mom.

"You are so ungrateful," I continued. "All that we ever want is the best for you, but all that you see is the bad in everything that we do."

"I am not ungrateful. But you have no right to let me stay here if I am fine," Mom said.

"Not until the doctor says you can be released will we take you home."

And with that, the little debate or rather argument was settled. I was fuming, knowing very well that Mom hated hospitals but feeling aggrieved that Mom could not see the urgency and the reason for taking her to hospital.

And for the next week, every night Mom would blame me and insist that she be released from hospital and I simply ignored her tirade. But Mom never relented, not until the day she finally was released from hospital. Taking Mom home, we ensured that she stayed inside, that she remained warm and refused to have her visiting Tranquillity for the remainder of the winter. It was tough on Mom, and she often reminded us that our commitment to her was that we would take her to Tranquillity whenever she felt like going. Mom played on our feelings, as only she knew how. And this was true, we had promised many years ago to ensure that Mom could go to Tranquillity, as often and whenever she wanted. And for the most part, we lived up to that promise and commitment but we had Mom's health in mind and therefore would not relent.

Finally, when spring arrived, and Mom completely recovered, Mom was once again dropped off at Tranquillity and life returned to its normal routine for Mom. We watched Mom very closely, always scared of a cough, but more scared of whether she had lost her appetite or whether she was in any pain. And all seemed well with Mom and she never once mentioned any pain or that she was unable to keep her food in. But living with the knowledge that Mom had cancer placed a huge burden of responsibility on Sis and I. But we simply had to endure it.

One day whilst sitting by the pool, Mom out of the blue mentioned to me that she thought she had cancer.

"We all have cancer, Mom. And you know it. Our cancer cells are merely dormant," I tried to steer away from the conversation.

"Look at the growth on the side of my head and the one on my back. It is getting worse."

"Let me see, please show me, Mom," I asked Mom.

Mom wore a patch on the side of her head to cover the growth, and when I looked at it, it seemed fine to me, same with the growth on her back. But I was no doctor.

"Would you like Sis to take you to the doctor so that the doctor could have a look at it?" I enquired.

"No!" Mom said. "I will not let them cut me open. I will not have any treatment."

"Then stop worrying about it," I said. "If it gets worse, then we will have to admit you to hospital. But until then, let's keep an eye on it."

By this time we also took out a hospital plan for Mom, so there was no need to be concerned in the event that we had to admit her to hospital financially. But this discussion just reiterated the way Mom felt about cancer, doctors and hospitals in general.

Several years passed since Mom was in hospital for pneumonia, and there was never any cause for hospitalisation again. Mom from time to time went to the doctor, as being in her seventies, she developed osteoporosis, she was anaemic and arthritic and she constantly lived with pain. But on every enquiry and every visit to the doctor we were assured that it was structural pain, pain in her brittle bones, but never pain in her stomach.

"I might as well die," Mom bemoaned the pain that she endured. This despite the fact that the doctor prescribed some pills which reduced Mom's pain and discomfort.

"Just don't die until I have turned forty!" I would tease Mom often, thinking to myself that sometimes Mom could also be quite the hypochondriac and have a flare for drama.

In the year of my fortieth birthday, Mom kept up her side of the agreement and continued to live up to my banter and her promise as she was fortunately still around, albeit that one could see the gradual decline in Mom. Hardship and many years of being worried, concerned, troubled and having an abusive husband all eventually had to take its toll on Mom. Mom constantly lived with pain, but again, only pain of a crumbling bone structure and not any pain related to her cancer.

One Friday late morning, a few months after my fortieth birthday, I attended a funeral of an old school friend whose mother had unexpectedly passed away. Her mother was also in the same congregation as I was so her mother was very well known to me. The funeral service was held in Tranquillity, as this was still where her mother stayed after all these years. The service was quite sad and touching, and attending the service, I ran into some of Mom's old friends and acquaintances, some of whom I have not seen in many years.

As the funeral service was held in the church right opposite where my aunt stayed, and Mom was dropped off that morning for her regular and customary visit. I knew that if Mom was at my aunt's and not by one of her other friends, that Mom would be standing around outside watching the mourners and family members and friends exit the church. On this day, I had a business lunch with some associates and I did inform them that I would be running late, as attending the funeral was a priority to me. Upon leaving the church, I did not see Mom, which I was surprised by, but also relieved, as I knew that Mom would stop me and wanted to have a brief chat. I simply could not stay, as I already had the associates kept waiting for more than an hour.

"Is my mom around?" I still asked one of the Tranquillity spectators who also knew Mom.

"No, she went down to the shop," the lady informed me. "I can go and call her for you."

"No! No! Please don't. I need to go as I have a meeting. Please don't let my mom know that I was here."

And with those words, I got in my car and drove to the lunch venue.

The next morning, five of my closest friends and I took a flight to KwaZulu-Natal as we were invited to attend a wedding. We left for the venue early on Saturday morning and upon arrival at Durban International Airport, we then took a rental car and drove the hour or so to the venue. We were quite excited at spending the weekend away and looked forward to a wonderful time at the wedding reception. We were booked into a lodge at the venue, so upon arrival we immediately got ready for the wedding, dressing up and making ourselves quite respectable. And what a beautiful and intimate wedding reception it was. Due to the venue, only a select few of the family members and friends were invited to attend the wedding, and we thoroughly enjoyed ourselves. We danced and partied until late in the evening and finally went to bed in the early hours of the morning, eager to get some shut eye as we were due to depart on Sunday afternoon for home again.

The lodge is in a remote location and cell phone signal was quite appalling. I did not mind the solitude of no phone calls, as we were surrounded by nature, we had a tent tree house and we had mild weather. All making for a wonderful time.

The next morning at six, I woke and started getting ready for our return trip. I looked at my cell phone and noticed that I still had no reception. I simply shrugged and knew the moment we left the venue; the problem would be something of the past. But one of my friends happened to have reception, and while I was busy in the bathroom, he walked into the bathroom and handed me his phone.

"I think you need to take this call," he said. Pale, ashen in fact and quite uncertain how to behave around me.

"Who is it?" I asked.

"Please take the call," he urged me. I took the cell phone from him, not sure how to read his body language.

"Hello?" I asked into the phone with a strange sense of foreboding.

Sis was on the other side of the telephone, and she was crying, sobbing, raw wails uttered from her.

"What is it? What is wrong?" I asked her, taking a seat on the side of the bath as my legs just simply would not support me.

"I…I think it is Mom," Sis said. "I think she has passed away."

Now Sis sometimes has an active mind that sometimes runs away with her. So I gathered my thoughts.

"Are you sure?" I asked her. "Where is Mom now?"

"In her room. She is all cold," Sis said.

"She will be, it is winter," I rationalised.

"No!" Sis wailed. "Mom is not breathing. I have called for assistance."

I realised that in between Sis' crying and trying to convey to me the saddest possible news ever that there were voices in the background, people who could, in fact, confirm that Sis was wrong.

"Are you sure?" I asked, but Sis was no longer on the phone. Family friends of ours went over immediately when they received the call from Sis, and they confirmed the harsh reality to me on the phone, six hundred kilometres away from home.

Oh dear God, no. O dear Lord, no. Not Mom. Not my mom. Please, dear Lord, I prayed. Please let this be wrong. Please, Lord. I need to see her one last time. I need to talk to her one last time.

I need to tell her one last time that I loved her. That I would never be able to thank her enough for all that she did for us over all the years of poverty and hardship. O, God, please. Let them all be wrong. Let them come back to me and say that she was only unconscious. Dear Lord, I beg thee. Not today. Not now. Not so soon.

I turned around, handed the phone back to my friend, saw the look on his sister's face and knew that she had also spoken to her family, and it was confirmed. No words were necessary any longer. No confirmation. I could see in her desolate and forlorn look that my wildest nightmare had come true.

Without a word, I walked out of the room, down the stairs unable to comprehend what has just happened. My other two close friends were still in their bungalow. I knocked and entered. Seeing them all of a sudden knocked the wind out of me, I doubled over and I started to scream.

"Mom is dead. O, dear God, no. Mom is dead."

My friends did not know what to do, or how to react, but they knew that all that I needed was comfort. And that they all bestowed onto me. And I kept on crying, crying for a mother who was my biggest supporter. Mom. Our family matriarch. Mom. Who fought poverty, who victoriously survived the onslaughts of life. Mom. My pillar of strength. My anchor. My fortress. Mom. O, Mom.

A little while later, my friends had packed all their and even my belongings and as per our plans for the weekend, we went to the local shopping centre for breakfast before going to the airport for our departure flight home. The conversation in the rental vehicle from the time that we left was subdued. I sat in front and knew that everyone was unsure of how to react. So I tried to be strong. I could not talk, not on the phone and not to anyone in the car. At one time, while the tears were running down my face, in order to not look back at my friends and making them more uneasy, I texted my one friend and asked her for a tissue. Without a word, she took a tissue out of her bag, realised that it was a private moment and surreptitiously handed me the tissue to wipe away my tears.

Upon arriving at the shopping centre, we decided on a restaurant to have breakfast. We entered the restaurant and as they had open tables outside overlooking a lake, we all opted to sit in the open, with the sun shining down upon us. As this was a franchise and I am a creature of habit, so when I frequent the same restaurant group on a regular basis, I will always have the same food. Today, my order was the same. We kept our conversation light, reflecting on the wedding rather than discussing the torment my soul was going through.

The food arrived, and everyone started to eat. I simply could not touch my food. I looked at it and realised that there was simply no way for me to be able to eat. I asked to be excused, I went to the bathroom, I sat down and started crying again. I am not sure how long I was in there, but when I walked out, I could see that my friends were extremely concerned about me. They understood that no words could comfort me; they understood that I had no appetite and they understood that all I wanted to do was get the day over and get home. So that I could deal with my loss.

The drive to the airport was as agonising as the drive from the venue. We booked in, awaited our flights and finally boarded the plane. Sis was not at home, so I arranged with Sis via text to meet her at my friends' house, the same family members who assisted Sis in her time of agony.

Strapped in my seat, I turned to my one friend and asked her if she would mind if I slept. I simply did not feel up to any conversation. I asked her also to please wake me if I started to drool, or if I snore. She was happy to oblige. An hour later, we arrived in

Johannesburg, took the train to our cars and I got in the car with the friends whose house I would meet up with Sis. My other two friends took my car and drove home.

The drive in the car was agonising. I did not speak; I only looked out the window as the landscape passed me by, not seeing anything. I was lost. Completely and utterly destroyed. I have never felt this way. I could never have imagined that it could hurt this much. I had no words. And I hated myself. Hated myself and blamed God for not allowing me one final goodbye with Mom. Had I not been in such a hurry to attend the business lunch, had I only taken the time to talk to Mom, I would at least have had the opportunity to know that I saw her shortly before her passing. No one could have foreseen that Mom would have a cerebral haemorrhage. But I loathed myself. I felt so guilty. What difference would another five minutes have made? Five minutes that I now coveted. That I wanted to relive and that I wanted to spend with Mom. Five minutes. But the Lord withheld this from me. "Why, Lord?" I asked in prayer.

Arriving at the friends' house, Sis' car was parked outside. I could not face any people. I simply could not go in. I stood outside and when I saw Sis, my soul was torn in two. Heartbroken, my soul was wrenched from me. Sis and I embraced and in the street, we both cried for a very long time. The only person I could speak to was Sis. I asked her to open the car and apologise for my behaviour, but I simply could not face anyone, not talk to anyone and I most definitely could not hear any words of sympathy or be consoled. All I wanted was for Sis and I to be alone, alone with our sorrow, alone with our loss, alone without Mom. And I knew that our friends understood this, that this was the only way I could cope with my grief.

Many friends and colleagues tried to call me that afternoon, as the ones at the venue were informed what happened, and they relayed the sad truth to others. But I simply could not talk to anyone and therefore refused to take any calls. I responded to each call with a text, letting them know I could not talk but that I was thankful for their support. Sis and I drove home, to her house. I needed to see Mom's room one last time the way she left it. Sis relayed what happened to me during our trip to her house, through tears and very faltering. I listened but did not have anything to offer in return.

Upon arriving at home, Sis started crying again, I never once stopped since getting in her car. We walked into the house and it was empty. Void. The kindest, best and most loving soul that we had ever known was gone. Has left this mortal coil and left us behind. I envied Sis, as she had spent Mom's last moments with Mom. I never had the chance to say goodbye.

Entering Mom's room, it was empty of her now. But her smell and her presence somehow lingered. I sat on the edge of Mom's bed, hoping for some warmth left behind in the impression on the mattress. Hoping against hope that this was a bad dream and that I will awake and find that everything is as it should be. But the dream never ended. It was reality.

Sis then showed me Mom's wedding ring and advised that the emergency service personnel had taken it off before they took Mom away.

"Would you mind if I ask you if I could have it?" I asked Sis.

"Of course not. It is yours," Sis said without hesitation.

I took the ring, I took my chain off that was around my neck and I attached the ring to the chain. And I promised Mom that I would never take it off. That her ring would beat close to my heart, and her ring would be comforting to me that I carried her in my heart and in my soul every day of my life.

After a while, we had to go and pick up my niece, who Sis took to family members, as she wanted my niece to be spared the ordeal of witnessing the handling of Mom's remains. My niece was nine years old and did not truly understand the concept of death. Again, I asked Sis to apologise on my behalf, but I did not leave the comfort of her car, I did not enter the house of our family members. Sis was not long, and my niece got in the back of the car. And even at that young and tender age, uncomprehending the circumstances but somehow she knew that words were unnecessary that I only craved their presence and their being there with me.

Sis and I then went to my place, where my two friends who took my car were also waiting for me. In Sis' mind at least I had companionship and would not be alone. When we arrived at home, Sis was eager to talk about what happened, she needed this, as this was therapeutic to her. I could not talk about it at all. After a while, Sis and my niece left and I asked to be excused, as I needed to take a shower. I would be going to work the next day. My friends objected, but I could not stay at home, I had to keep my mind busy and I simply had to get away from it all. I still was not hungry but managed to eat a slice of toast. I then went upstairs and got in the shower. Whilst in the shower, another burst of sorrow overcame me, and I cried, sinking to my knees, with the hot water pelting me, I continued to cry until I heaved. And eventually, I got out of the shower and climbed in bed.

Mom was cremated the Friday, and a private memorial ceremony was held. Private in the sense that there was no coffin, it was a memorial service for friends and family members who knew and loved Mom and wanted to honour her memory one last time. I did not want anyone from work to attend Mom's funeral, simply for me, it was a very private and deeply sorrowful day, and I did not want anyone who did not know Mom to experience this with me. Sis, on the other hand, needed all the support she could get from her work friends and colleagues, and requested their attendance if they felt like supporting her.

From the time I was called by Sis and every day thereafter, even after the memorial service, I kept on talking to the Lord needing to understand why the Lord kept me away from Mom on that Friday. Why, when the Lord knew that he would take Mom that fateful Sunday, why that Friday when I had the opportunity to talk to her, he allowed me to let it go. And I never received an answer. And in my prayers, I asked the Lord, if I could only have one last conversation with Mom. To only hear her voice one last time. And this time around, the Lord smiled upon me. For the one evening, a few weeks after the service, for the first time, I dreamt of Mom. The remnants of the dream I can never recall, I cannot recall the words, but I heard Mom's voice. And Mom was laughing.

***

Drained, I stood up from the bay window and noticed it started to rain again. And as the raindrops ran down the window, so did the tears again stream down my face. To this day, six years later, I am unable to talk to anyone about how I feel about Mom's death. I cannot describe my guilt, my anger, my confusion around what happened, and why it happened. For the last six years, Mom's ring has never been taken off the chain around my neck. Every day I think of Mom. Every single day. Every morning I kiss her wooden urn, in the form of a coffin that holds some of her ashes, as the others were placed in the wall of remembrance, together with Sasha's ashes. They are finally together again.

Every second Sunday for the last six years Sis and I visit Mom's wall of remembrance. We will replace the flowers with a fresh bunch, I will clean her wall stone, and Sis will arrange the flowers. We will talk to Mom, and I never leave without kissing Mom goodbye.

And today, I again realised how deep my loss was. How much I miss Mom. How she was the compass that steered me in life, without the need of saying anything. Mom. Who accepted me for who I was, loved me unconditionally and never ever humiliated me. Mom who fought for me, who believed in me, who loved me, who cared for me.

Losing Mom was one of the most soul-destroying experiences I ever had. That hole has never healed. Time does indeed attempt to heal all wounds, but sometimes partial healing only takes place and it doesn't mean it is necessarily better. I have learned to cope with not having Mom in my life. And indeed, over time, it has become more bearable. There will always be a void, always be a loss. I will never heal. Time has softened the rawness, the hurt, the damage. But it can never make it better. It is but one other hole in my soul that runs so deep that it will never mend. And I have learned to accept that this is the way it will be until my dying day. And that my soul will forever remain scarred.

I looked at my watch and realised that time indeed has flown by on this day. A day that started with a dream followed by lyrics from a song and ended with a floodgate of memories opened to unleash the inner storm within me. Drained, tired, unsure of why I had to walk back in time to meet up with the present again. Walking back in my footsteps and reliving the past, looking for absolution, for the release of all the hurt that was trapped by my soul. That I avoided and never confronted. And that it finally has caught up with me. That this was what was needed before I could continue again.

I switched off the lights, the air conditioner and went to my room. It has stopped raining, I realised although it was still bitterly cold. I got into bed, under the warm blankets and simply closed my eyes and almost immediately fell asleep. But not before I hoped and prayed that if I dream that it would not be a repeat of the turmoil I faced today. And then I slipped down the dark tunnel of dreams, into darkness and into rest.

Epilogue:
The Soul Healers

woke up the next morning, slowly opening my eyes, looking out the window. It is no longer raining, but it remains a cold and bleak day. What a strange day I had yesterday, I thought to myself. But waking up this morning, despite the cold, despite the deadly grip of winter all around me, I felt as if a burden has been lifted from my shoulders. Strangely, I felt lighter.

I stood up, yawned, stretched and went into the bathroom. I showered, I brushed my teeth and I went downstairs. I unlocked the door, got in my car and drove to the nearest shopping centre. There I first had breakfast, all by myself, with a cup of steaming hot chocolate and foam. I then went in search of the CD with those special lyrics. And I found it. I walked to my car, inserted the CD into my CD player in the car, scanned for the track and set the CD player on repeat. The song was playing over and over again. And every time I listened to the song, I became lighter still, featherweight and knew that I have come to peace with myself. That the holes in my soul will be there forever, some deep, others superficial, but each hole was a lesson, some of them seemingly unnecessary whilst others still very important in moulding the clay it is working with. The end result is who and what I am today.

Sated, not only by the breakfast but also by being able to listen to the lyrics and knowing that I have come to terms with my past, with what had shaped me, meandering along in my life until the sculpture is complete. Complete up to this point, to this day and time in my life. And knowing that the Sculptor will continue to sculpt, to poke holes, to chisel, to etch. And this all makes you who you are today.

Driving home, with the recurring song and its lyrics blasting in my ears, I sang along. And I loved the song. At home, I logged onto iTunes, I bought and downloaded the song, so that in future wherever I go, it will be with me. On a CD, on my iPod or on my iPhone. And I could listen to it at will.

So how many holes can there be in a soul before a soul is destroyed, I started to ponder. And looking back at more than four decades of life, of living, of pain, suffering, poverty, soul-ache, heartache, disappointment, ridicule, misery and death, I accepted that these are the tools used by the Sculptor to sculpt us. And that each of us has a choice in life. And at each choice, each junction, each crossroads, we make decisions that shape the rest of our journeys, and the Sculptor either uses more tools at His disposal or continues to use that which was already set aside for the journey in the first place.

And that through shaping you, the holes carved into your soul are always countered with blessings that enrich your soul. That your soul will not always only have holes, but mostly that for each hole you have countless blessings. That I was able to love and be loved. That although I have a few very close friends, I have many good friends who all are part of my life. That people most of the times accept me for who and what I am. That people and friends like spending time with me. That they enjoy me, my sense of humour, my direct approach, my no-nonsense attitude, my reasoning, my ability to argue and debate, never to back down when believing in a cause. That my friends, my family and my loved ones know that when I give, I do so unconditionally. The gift of love, the gift of acceptance, the gift of time. One hundred per cent every time. All the time.

Sitting in the bay window, looking at the leafless trees, the cold day outside, listening to the howling wind, I realised that my life could have been so different. I could have chosen the road of poverty, I could have chosen the temptation of alcohol, I could have used the poor examples set to me by a father who lacked being a parent, I could have chosen to drop out of school. But I didn't. And neither did Sis. That we aspired to a better life, a different life, a life so unlike the one we lived when we were children. And that our own children would never want for anything in life, not while we could prevent it with every fibre of our beings.

My faith has carried me through this all my life. My love for my family and my friends has been my safety net, my pillars of strength. That the path to true happiness is different for each of us. Some have it easy for their entire lives, others not so much. But the journey and the experiences are all different. And these mould our souls. And heal our souls. Never entirely. But somewhat. I have a hole in my soul. One created by so many life experiences. But my soul is all the better for it. Wholesome. Free. And I no longer wore poverty and labels as an invisible chain that threatened to drag me down. I stood up and dusted myself off every time. And that I needed to relive it, to experience it again to understand how to tackle the journey going forward.

I stood up, in the mood for conversation. I went downstairs again, got in my car and drove away, eager to see what experiences this day and every day hereafter will bring. And that I will embrace these, the good, the bad, the sad, the happy. It makes no difference. For my Sculptor has not finished sculpting me yet.

The End